Just a Cowboy's Love Story

Flyboys of Sweet Briar Ranch in North Dakota
Book Five
Jessie Gussman

Published By: Jessie Gussman

Contents

Acknowledgements

Cover art by Julia Gussman
Editing by Heather Hayden
Narration by Jay Dyess
Author Services by CE Author Assistant

Listen to a FREE professionally performed and produced audiobook version of this title on Youtube. Search for "Say With Jay" to browse all available FREE Dyess/Gussman audiobooks.

Chapter 1

"I guess we're going to have to do this on our own," Sorrell said, sitting on the ground, forming a triangle with her sister and her friend making up the other corners.

"We're just kids. What are we going to be able to do?" Merritt, her sister, said, using a stick to dig in the dirt. She had gotten quite a hole dug, four inches deep or so. Which, considering it was an old, abandoned lot behind their mom's diner in Sweet Water, North Dakota, wasn't too shabby.

"Lots of times, kids can do a lot," Sorrell said, but she knew her tone wasn't very confident. She was only ten. How was she going to find a husband for her mom and a dad for herself and her sister when she was only ten?

Her friend, Toni, who was also ten, didn't seem to be paying attention to their conversation.

Her mom was also unmarried, and she hadn't even known her dad.

She didn't talk about it too much, but Sorrell was pretty sure her mom got pregnant before she graduated from high school, and the father hadn't wanted to have a kid.

Toni understood Sorrell and Merritt's predicament, even though Sorrell and

Merritt had vague memories of their dad, since he and their mom had gotten divorced when they were just little.

"No wonder she likes to hang out behind the diner so much. Your mom's always burning things and sending one of us out to throw things in her pan."

"Is that what you're looking at?" Sorrell said, twisting around until she saw Munchy snorting happily at her food pan.

She hadn't even noticed. She'd been deep in thought about how they could figure out how to match their mom up.

She wanted to snap at her friend, tell her to pay attention and think of something.

But a lot of times, Toni was thinking when she didn't seem to be paying attention.

"We helped the three old men. Their video was at 1.3 million views the last I saw it. They wouldn't have had that without us," Merritt said, and she still seemed to be latched onto the idea that the three old men who took cooking classes at the diner were somehow going to help them find a man for their mom.

Sorrell had given up on that idea the second Mr. Marshall suggested Paul as a potential match. There was no way. If that was who those men thought would be a good husband for her mom, she wasn't the slightest bit interested in getting any more names from them. She'd do without a dad before she wanted a dad like that.

That didn't mean she wasn't going to help the old men.

They'd made a promise, and she had to keep her promise. The men had kept their end of the bargain, giving them a name. Just because Sorrell didn't like the name didn't mean she got out of her end of the deal.

The deal was that the men would give them a potential match for their mom, and she and her friends would help them use TikTok and set up videos that people would want to watch.

And they had. If 1.3 million views were any indication.

"Although, that video isn't really helping them, because they're not getting anyone they can talk to. They're just views and likes and some comments," Merritt said, her brows crinkled.

"I know. But it's dangerous to put your address up on social media."

That was the only video they'd made so far. The men had suggested they make one letting the ladies know where they needed to go, but Sorrell had dragged her feet at that suggestion.

Her mom had always said that social media could be dangerous, and while she wasn't sure exactly what anyone would do to hurt the old men, she did know there were some pretty crazy people in the world.

"Incoming!" Toni shouted, jumping up and scrambling to the side, grabbing Merritt's and Sorrell's hands as she did so, dragging them along with her.

Sorrell stumbled to her feet, taking big steps trying to catch her balance as Toni dragged her away.

Beside her, she could see Merritt having the same issue, and at one point, Toni pulled her through the dirt with both of her legs dragging.

Pounding hooves made it clear that Toni hadn't been exaggerating the danger, and she wouldn't be dragging Merritt over the dirt if it weren't serious.

By the time they managed to get about twenty yards from where they'd been sitting, Toni stopped and turned around.

Sorrell stopped with her and turned just in time to see Munchy storming by while Billy, the Highlander cow who roamed around Sweet Water, chased the hog just as fast as his stubby legs could go.

He wasn't a miniature, but he must have been some kind of cross, because he wasn't as big as a normal steer.

No one knew who owned either one of the animals, but the town had gotten together to make sure they had feed and water on a daily basis in the lot behind the diner.

It just so happened to be the lot that Sorrell and Merritt and Toni normally hung out in when they weren't in school.

It was kind of like their hideout, only they were in plain sight of anyone who went behind the first row of houses in town. The ones that lined Main Street.

"I don't understand why Billy is always chasing Munchy." Toni shook her head, looking over at Merritt. "I'm sorry. I knew we needed to get out of there. You know how they are when Billy gets his eye set on Munchy."

"It's okay," Merritt said, brushing off the knees of her jeans where they dragged in the dirt and were now dusty. "That's not the first time I almost got trampled. I'm glad you grabbed a hold of me and pulled. I might have gotten in their way."

"Billy's so gentle. I can't believe he'd run over you, but I think Munchy would eat you if she could." Sorrell didn't have a whole lot of time for pigs. They smelled bad.

"She's sweet. I don't know why you always have such a hard time with her," Toni said, looking after the pig. "I scratch her a lot, and she loves it. She even lies down beside me."

"I've heard pigs are really smart."

"Munchy is. But she can't seem to shake Billy."

"That makes Billy the dumb one. He doesn't seem to understand that he's not a pig," Toni pointed out

"Or he doesn't understand that Munchy isn't a cow."

"He's a steer. He shouldn't be interested in female cows anyway. Female any things."

"Well, you saw what I did, and we all know that Billy isn't chasing her to be mean to her. He's chasing her because he likes her," Toni said, brushing off some dirt that Merritt had missed on her jeans.

Toni was almost as much of a big sister to Merritt as Sorrell was.

Sorrell knew Toni wanted little brothers and sisters of her own. Kids she could play with and take care of and mother. The way she loved to do.

Sometimes at school when Sorrell heard people complaining about their siblings, she wondered why God gave siblings to some people and didn't give them to others.

"It's too bad we can't get whatever Munchy uses to attract Billy and give it to our mom," Merritt said as she stepped back over to where they'd been sitting.

Toni laughed. "Or give it to some man who comes in the diner so your mom will actually notice a man. She's so busy working, she doesn't pay attention to anything other than her job."

"And us. She pays attention to us."

"Yeah. But that's what moms are supposed to do."

"Not all moms do."

"I know. But she doesn't get credit for paying attention to her kids. And she would get credit for paying attention to her husband, because it's extra. She needs to get her nose out of her kids and her business and start paying attention to the men around here. They're getting snatched up so fast we barely get a hold of one and somebody else has married him." Toni plopped back down on the ground, leaning back and lying down in the dirt.

But Sorrell was thinking.

Was there something to that?

She looked over at the food pan.

It was true that Munchy ate a lot of her mom's food. Could it be something in her mom's cooking?

Her mom was always looking for perfect recipes. Recipes that people loved and would come back for. Recipes that made them feel happy when they were done eating. Recipes that warmed them from the tips of their toes to the tops of their heads and made them feel content and satisfied and like eating was a pleasure.

She joked that she wanted them to have good memories of coming in the diner. And since it was kind of old and raggedy looking, the only thing she could do was to make the food so good they didn't notice how old and ugly and run down everything else looked.

Was it possible her food somehow made Munchy appealing to Billy?

That Munchy ate the food, and she no longer looked old and raggedy to Billy, but fun and happy and appealing, and Billy just wanted to be with her?

Sorrell bit her lip.

Was it possible that they could tweak one of her mom's recipes just a little? Tweak it enough that a man would eat it and her mom wouldn't be able to take her eyes off him?

Maybe it wasn't just eating it one time. Maybe they needed to find a man who would eat it every day.

She wasn't sure. Didn't know if maybe there was a special blend of ingredients that might work.

It seemed Munchy had found the secret. Or had eaten the secret. Or something.

"Hey, do you girls want to come play baseball?" Owen came around the side of the building, tossing a ball up with his right hand and catching it with the mitt that covered his left.

"They just want us because they don't have enough boys to make up the team. They wouldn't ask us if they had guys who could take our place," Toni muttered, and she didn't look inclined to want to go.

"Were we doing something else?" Sorrell asked, with her brows raised. After all, who cared why they'd asked. It just mattered that they did.

"I like his sister. She's nice," Merritt said, standing up. "And usually they have her playing."

"Come on, Toni, don't be so prickly," Sorrell said, sitting up and bumping her friend's shoulder with her own.

"All right. But we have to keep thinking about this. There's got to be something we can do. I want a dad."

She knew she sounded a little bit demanding, but it was true. Everybody else had a dad, except for Toni, and she wanted one too. She wanted someone who would teach her how to play baseball, so when the guys asked her to play, they didn't make fun of her for throwing like a girl and not being able to hit the ball.

"You will. We're working on it. And God wouldn't want us all to grow up without a dad, so we can be sure He's going to give us one. We just have to wait until He finds the right guy." Merritt hadn't said much, and her words were soft.

"God hasn't lost anyone. He knows exactly where everyone is. He could send one any time." Sorrell didn't mean to be impatient, and she definitely didn't want to be sacrilegious, but she was of the mind that if she wanted a dad, she'd better go get one and give God a little bit of help with His job.

Maybe that wasn't quite the attitude she should have, but she kind of thought if she waited on God, she'd never get a dad.

She stood, brushing her butt off so the boys didn't make fun of her for having dirt on it, and followed her friends around the corner to the new ballpark the town had put in not long ago.

She tucked away the idea of a secret sauce, or elixir, or something, to use at some point.

Better yet, she had an idea.

"Merritt, Toni. Wait."

Toni looked a little annoyed, but she stopped and turned around with her hands on her hips. "If they start playing before we get there, they probably won't let us join."

"I won't take long. I just have an idea. When we're not busy and not playing baseball or going to school, I want you to stake out the diner." She looked at her little sister. She was cute with blue eyes and curly blonde hair, and adults were always talking about what an adorable little girl she was.

"Stake out the diner? What do you mean?"

"I mean, men come in here, they're not married, and before we can grab them for ourselves, the town matchmakers get them matched up with someone else, or someone snatches them up before we get a chance. We need to find a man, and we need to get to him before anybody else does. Got that?"

"All right," Merritt said, still looking a little unsure, but Merritt was nothing if not tenacious, and if Sorrell told her to stake out the diner, she wouldn't leave her post, even if she wasn't sure what she was supposed to be doing at that post.

"And you." She pointed to Toni. "I want you to stake out the rest of the town. Same deal. If a man comes in and he's not married, you're going to pounce on him. You call in the reinforcements—that's us—" she said, looking at Merritt and herself.

"I knew that," Toni said.

"And we'll figure out how to get him before anyone else does. Okay?"

"All right," Toni said, not sounding like she believed the plan was going to be any better than any of the other plans that they'd had, but at least it was a plan.

"What are you going to do?" Toni asked, crossing her hands over her chest and looking at Sorrell.

"I am going to search the Internet for love potions."

Chapter 2

Elias Stone rolled down the dirt lane, a little frustrated with himself.

He was on his way to Sweet Briar Ranch, and the last house he'd seen must have been ten minutes back at least.

Could his crew have found a more desolate place to buy a ranch?

Of course, he supposed they all wanted to be out of civilization as much as they could, so it made sense that they looked for a place in an area that wasn't very populated, but he was pretty sure they'd found the most sparsely populated state in the country.

Antarctica might have been slightly more desolate. But honestly, he wasn't even sure about that.

Even though it was only October, a cold wind blew, sweeping up a bunch of dead grass and stubble and blowing it across the driveway.

That wind was going to be brutal in winter with nothing to stop it.

He'd been stationed in Montana for years and knew that it got cold there, but he'd heard that North Dakota was even worse.

Still, the cold didn't really matter to him.

Nothing really mattered, to be honest.

He'd been court-martialed and found guilty because he couldn't present the evidence that would prove his innocence, because he'd promised he wouldn't tell.

To him, a promise was something a man kept no matter what.

He'd been dishonorably discharged, which had ruined the entire plan he had for his life.

It was hard not to be bitter.

Especially because the person who knew the truth, the person he'd made that promise to, could have stepped up. But they didn't. Because it would have incriminated them.

He swallowed, pulling his Jeep to a stop beside the two pickups that already sat there.

He supposed he'd have to be trading his Jeep in on a pickup, if he was going to become a rancher.

He couldn't dredge up much enthusiasm for that, either. Any more enthusiasm than he had been able to dredge up for anything over the last year since the court-martial and dishonorable discharge had gone down.

He hadn't been going to come here, but he'd been living with his mom and stepdad, and his presence in the house had been putting a strain on their marriage.

His stepdad hadn't wanted to keep putting up with the bum son who'd come back disgraced.

So, he packed his bags, took the little bit that he had, and headed out west to join his crew.

Apparently, they felt there was room for him out here.

He looked around, another gust of wind almost knocking him sideways. He huffed out a laugh. There was definitely room. For what, he wasn't sure, but there was room.

He finished walking up the four steps and rapped on the door, waiting a few seconds before he walked in.

"You guys home?" he yelled into the interior as he walked in.

"Hey! Elias? You're here!" Gideon jumped up from the recliner where he'd been sitting and shoved his phone in his pocket before hurrying across and wrapping Elias in a bear hug.

Elias wasn't much for touchy-feely things, which was part of the reason he hadn't wanted to come here to be with his crew.

There were a lot of memories associated with these guys, and he would have to fight through them in order to make a life here.

Not to mention, he'd been the commanding officer, and he thought that might make things a little tricky too. He didn't want to be someone who was in charge anymore. Who would have to make decisions or boss people around. He just wanted to have a no-brainer job, and a no-brainer life, and have plenty of time to think about how things weren't fair.

That wasn't entirely true. He wanted to put the past behind him, but he didn't want to put it behind and yet still be constantly reminded of his life in the Air Force.

"How was your trip in?" Gideon asked as he stepped back so Jonah could shake his hand.

Jonah was always a little more reserved than Gideon. Gideon was always ready with a smile, and if there was any goofing off going down, he was in the middle of it.

"Windy. I don't think I've ever seen wind like this before. Not even in Montana."

"Montana's a completely different animal than North Dakota," Jonah said, narrowing his eyes at Elias, as though wondering whether he was really okay.

He supposed his court-martial would be the elephant in the room. The details that had been leaked to the public were few and far between.

There was one nice thing about the military.

It had all been in-house. If it had been public, everyone would have known everything.

Which, since everything wasn't actually everything, it would make him look terrible.

"I believe it from the little I've seen," he said, automatically resisting the urge to pivot and walk right back out of the house. He had his feet planted, his duffel in hand, and forced himself to stand still.

"Come on. I'll show you to your room," Gideon said, smacking his arm and turning toward the steps.

Elias followed without comment, feeling like this was the worst idea he'd had in a really long time. Of course, it had been a long time since he'd had any kind of idea that had sounded like a good one and also turned out to be a good one.

He walked across the living room floor, which felt a little drafty to him, and he wondered how the house was going to keep them all warm when it actually got really cold. It was below freezing at that moment, but winter cold was often below zero in North Dakota.

"Jonah and I both have a bedroom to ourselves, and there are three more. Zeke and Baker are coming out in the spring, I think, so you get to choose."

"I don't care. I'll take whatever's available." It'd always been his policy that his crew members came before himself.

He supposed it was just something that he thought about so often that it was a natural thing.

"Great. If you don't care, I'll stick you in the bedroom next to mine," Gideon said with a grin like having Elias sleeping next to him was some kind of honor or something.

He tried not to roll his eyes at that. What a joke. It wasn't any honor. It was a dishonor—because of his dishonorable discharge—to even have him around.

He tried not to think that way. After all, he'd stuck to his convictions and hadn't told the secret he'd sworn not to. It had been a verbal promise; it hadn't even been any kind of legally binding document.

A man he'd thought was a friend had confided something to him and asked him not to say anything. He'd told him that he wouldn't.

It had been tempting to break that promise, it would have saved his bacon, but his career wasn't worth his integrity.

So, he no longer had a career, and his integrity felt rather cold right now.

In future years, he figured he would probably be happy that he had done what he did, but that point hadn't come yet. Not in a big way, even though in a small way, he knew he would handle everything exactly the same way if he had to do it over again.

But it was done and over with and nothing was going to change it. He wasn't even trying. He didn't care. Sometimes in life, things just stood. Things that were unfair, things that weren't right, things that shouldn't have happened. There was no resolution, no happy ending, no fairness. You just had to give it to God and walk away, living life as best you could.

That's what he thought, and that's what he would be doing.

"We take turns cooking. And take turns doing the dishes. We don't do too much cleaning, but we try to clean up after ourselves."

"That's fine." He didn't like dirt, and he'd probably end up doing a little more cleaning than the rest of the guys. But it didn't matter. He didn't like to clean, but he didn't hate it. And he didn't mind, because if the dirt bothered him, it just made sense that he would do something about it.

Gideon continued talking as he opened the door to the room Elias would be staying in. "Tomorrow, Jonah and I are going to an agricultural convention in the Cities. We've got space rented for a booth, and we're going to try to drum up some business for next year. We assumed if you got here in time, you'd be going with us."

Elias put his bag down on the floor, looked at the lone window in the room, saw that there was at least one blanket on the bed, and noticed the small dresser. Nothing fancy. The floor sloped slightly to the north, but he was out of the wind, and there'd be a little bit of heat anyway.

It would do.

"If you don't mind, I think I'll just stay here. It was a long drive, and I don't think

I want to pack up and go on another long drive tomorrow."

"That's fine. If you don't feel like cooking, you can always run into town. There's a diner there, and it's open until eight, ten on weekends, and sometimes later depending on business in the summer."

"All right. That's good to know."

Gideon rattled off a bunch of other information, where the nearest grocery store was, hardware stores, and their neighbors, as they walked back down the stairs.

Gideon and Jonah talked all through supper about the different plans that they had for the ranch.

Elias appreciated them trying to include him, but he just felt a little melancholy.

It wasn't that he resented the move. He just...needed to acclimate. Or maybe he wanted to branch out on his own a little. He didn't want to be in their business just for the sake of them including him. After all, he didn't really have anything to contribute.

He didn't know anything about agriculture, or raising or spraying crops, insecticides, nor whatever else they were talking about.

The only thing he could do was fly an airplane and work on them some, too.

Of course, that's all they could do when they came out, and they'd jumped in, pitching in on the work to get them-selves set up as a crop-dusting service. He supposed he should show a little more excitement about it, but he just had a hard time getting himself motivat-ed to do more than nod and try to focus on not looking bored.

"All right, we already told you that we'll be gone for three days, but if you need anything, you can always text us. Or if you have any questions. We have a key hanging on a hook beside the front door. If you weren't going to be here, we'd probably lock the house when we left for the Cities, but we never lock it when we just leave to go to town or something." Gideon shrugged. "I know it's crazy, but no one locks their doors around here."

"Maybe I can get some keys made. I think we ought to be locking them," Elias said, knowing that unspoken etiquette pretty much demanded that the new guy didn't come in and start making changes right away.

But after being in the military, he had a tendency to be suspicious, and the idea of not locking his door didn't sit well with him.

As he figured, neither one of the other two men at the table said anything. They wouldn't want to argue with him.

He reminded himself to keep his mouth shut and to learn what he need-ed to learn in order to fit in here.

This was a new start, and it would only be as good as what he made it. He had to remember that.

Yesterday had passed, and all the things that happened couldn't be undone, and he just had to live with them.

Plus, he'd promised himself that coming out here was going to be a new start between him and the Lord. He'd left the religion of his youth, and while the character lessons that he'd been taught had been reinforced by the military, the relationship that he was supposed to be having with God had been sadly neglected by him.

He'd thought he could do everything himself.

He'd been wrong.

Chapter 3

"I need hamburgers out of the big freezer in the back, lettuce, onions, a bottle of salad dressing, and I need to go to the pantry and get more flour, more salt, and more garlic."

Jane talked to herself, firming the list in her head so she wouldn't forget. She couldn't go get everything that second, because she had three tables that needed to be cleaned off since there were people standing in the doorway waiting to sit down.

Her phone buzzed, and she hoped it was Lya.

Lya was someone she wouldn't normally hire, since she'd only communicated via text so far, and she had stated that she didn't want to start working before noon, because she typically didn't get out of bed until eleven, and she'd also said that she didn't want to work more than six hours a day, that she wasn't sure what she wanted to be in life, but she'd already been a tattoo artist, a kayak instructor, had lived in a nudist compound, and had worked for one day on a construction crew.

Her texts were long and involved, and honestly, Jane usually didn't have time to read them until she got home and had put her children to bed.

Lya's questionable work ethic and her inability to stick with anything would have been bad enough, but so far, out of the four times Lya had told Jane that she was going to start working, she had backed out every time.

Once it had been because she was sick, which Jane could totally understand. But the second time, she said that her car broke down, which, again, was something Jane could totally understand.

The third time was because she decided to take a different job as a manicurist, which apparently hadn't lasted long, because two days after that, she told Jane she was coming back and was ready to start, and then she asked Jane if Jane could give her gas money so that she could make a trip to the grocery store before she came in to work.

Jane hadn't answered that text.

But Lya had texted again today. It just so happened that Jane's one remaining waitress was out sick, and her short-order cook had quit yesterday as well.

Jane was trying to manage the cash register, bus tables, and help the cook. Hence her list of things she needed to get out of the back refrigerator.

Her feet hurt, and so did her back, and she was trying to keep an eye on her girls, but she could only see Merritt, who sat on this side of the counter, in front of the seven or so stools that made up the bar counter portion of the diner.

Merritt was only nine, and Jane wouldn't allow her to do a whole lot of work, but she'd been cleaning off the counter and wiping it every time someone got up.

Jane appreciated it, because she really needed the help.

"I've been waiting a long time for my meal. Is it going to be out today? Because in this amount of time, I could have driven to Rockerton," said an older gentleman, possibly in his fifties, as she hurried by his table, intending to clean off the table beside his.

"I'm sorry. We're a little short-staffed today. I'm hoping in just a few minutes, I'll get someone to come in and give us a hand," she said, smiling, even though she didn't feel like it. "I'll check the kitchen as soon as I get back in there, and ask Peter about your order, okay?" She smiled again, hoping to look endearing but probably just looking frazzled. "I do apologize."

The man pressed his lips together, but he didn't berate her.

Some men had, and one woman had gotten up and left after spouting a lot of insults and vulgarities at Jane, like the slow service was something she could do something about.

Didn't they think that she would have if she could?

She got to the table, with her pan for the dishes and a rag, and stopped to check her texts. Lya had indeed sent a message, in response to Jane's reply to her text that whenever she could make it, she would be welcome.

I'm coming right in.

As many jobs as Lya had had, hopefully it wouldn't take her too long to get the hang of waitressing.

It wasn't that hard. Even their check-out system was super simple. She hadn't wanted to put a whole lot of money into upgrades when she wasn't sure whether she could make the diner profitable or not.

Being by herself, not having another reliable source of income, made her scared, drove her to work as hard as she could to try to make as much money as she could because she didn't want to lose her home. She had no safety net. Where was she going to go? What was she going to do? How was she going to support her daughters?

That was the biggest thing that she feared.

Not being able to have a safe place for her girls. So, she drove herself to work as hard as she could. Developing recipes, creating the best customer experience she possibly could, and making things simple and quick.

Not today.

She shoved her phone back in her pocket and cleared off the table, throwing the dirty dishes in the pan and wiping the tabletop and seats.

Even though she was rushed, she took her time, moving the salt and pepper and ketchup bottles around, making sure she wiped under them, giving the booth seats a good scrub, and looking to make sure she didn't miss anything on the floor.

Sliding her pan to the edge of the table, throwing the rag on top of the dirty dishes, she grabbed it and hurried back to the kitchen.

Except, her eyes caught on a tall man who walked in, the bell jingling over his head.

Dark, with deep brown eyes and dark brown hair, he looked intimidating. He carried himself with a straight back, a posture that almost screamed ex-military.

Or maybe current, although he wasn't dressed in fatigues.

They had a lot of those go through. North Dakota was a very patriotic state, and she always gave military men a discount. Sometimes she gave them their meal free, if they seemed like they needed a smile or pick-me-up.

This guy was different. There was something about him that made her want to put her hand over her stomach and quiet what felt like a riot of elephants in there.

Her hands tingled as she gripped the tub, and her feet, for some odd reason, wanted to walk toward him, rather than toward the kitchen.

He surveyed the diner like he was looking for something or someone, and she almost gave herself permission to walk toward him.

But she didn't have time. She didn't know that man, didn't recognize him at all, and would only be wasting her time if she left all the work that needed to be done to go talk to him. So she didn't.

Shaking her head, she hurried into the kitchen, setting the dirty dishes down, checking on the man's meal, and then running to the back freezer and refrigerator to get the things out that she needed.

Normally, she loved her job, loved what she did, loved her days, and didn't mind the feeling of needing to make it all work in order to provide a roof for her children, but today, she was tired.

Maybe she should think about selling the diner and finding a different job.

Chapter 4

Elias surveyed the diner, the door closing behind him.

It was colder this afternoon than it had been the night before, and he had a feel-ing that it was going to get worse before it got better.

As was his custom when he walked into a room, he stopped and checked it out, looking for anything that seemed out of place.

Maybe it was his years in the military that had trained him to be prepared for any situation, or maybe because it had been his responsibility, being in charge of a crew of men, their lives in his hands.

Maybe it had been the hostage situation he had been involved in, where he had been afraid that he would have his first fatalities, on home soil, no less.

It had resolved as well as could be hoped for, but it had marked him and was most likely the reason that he insisted the doors needed to be locked in their house.

One never knew when something was going to happen. It just happened. Therefore, it was best to do everything in one's power to be prepared.

He was getting ready to walk to one of the tables that were not cleaned off, when he saw a woman rushing by.

She slowed as her eyes met his, just for a second, and he felt something odd feather softly through his body.

Something like life.

Maybe two years ago, he wouldn't have noticed it.

But it was almost an electrical current that made the parts of him that felt dead inside toggle to life.

Rise and stretch and open their eyes.

He didn't exactly feel alive, but he felt...something.

The woman wasn't beautiful. Her hair was a mess, piled up on top of her head like she'd done it in a hurry, and there were dark circles under her eyes, like she'd been up since three o'clock in the morning and needed a break.

Odd he would think that, but even odder that he would want to be the one to tell her to sit down, to rest, that he'd help.

He hadn't come out to North Dakota to get involved with a woman and certainly not with a waitress. That hadn't been his intent at all.

He castigated himself for even being tempted to...what? Take the pan from her? Lead her to a table and tell her to sit? Ask her what she was doing and beg her to allow him to do it for her?

That was all ridiculous.

The moment passed, the woman hurried on, and he continued to survey the room.

She had just cleared off a table apparently, and someone had already sat in it.

He saw two more tables that needed to
be cleared, and his eyes tracked back to
the woman who was disappearing into
the kitchen to set down her pan of dirty
dishes.

He laughed a little to himself.

He could follow her into the kitchen,
grab the container, and go back out and
clear off his own table.

He'd started to take one step toward
the table when he thought, why not?

If it was so relaxed around Sweet Water
that no one locked their doors, surely
it wouldn't be considered a crime to go
back and get the tub from the kitchen so

he could clean up the table so he could sit down and have supper.

He hadn't eaten anything all day, waiting to go into town as long as possible, not wanting to meet people. He wouldn't mind becoming a hermit.

And more than that, the thought crossed his mind that if he was going to be dealing with the cold, he might as well deal with it in Antarctica.

Except, since he had been dishonorably discharged, it probably wouldn't be possible. He was pretty sure that a person didn't get to go to Antarctica unless they were part of some kind of government agency. Which he would never be.

Deciding that he'd rather have quick service so he could get in and get out, rather than sitting and waiting for someone to clear off the table in front of him, he changed his direction, pointing his steps toward the kitchen.

A little girl who'd been sitting behind the counter, the one he'd noticed on both sweeps his gaze had taken of the room, eyed him with interest as he walked past the cash register through the little walkway and behind the counter.

"Are you Lya?" she asked.

He jerked his head, not agreeing to her statement but just acknowledging her words.

"Mom is going to die. She'll be so glad you're here."

"I was going to go get the tub and clear off that table," he said, jerking his head toward the table he'd been planning to sit at. Could she really think he was some kind of new hire or something?

He didn't want to give that impression.

Did he look like he was a waitress?

Impossible. The girl was sitting there, comfortable and at ease, like she was there a lot. She would recognize the hired help.

"Awesome," the girl said, jumping up and hurrying in front of him.

He must have been right. People in this small town really did take casual to a whole new level.

Hopefully the prices of the food reflected the fact that patrons had to clear off their own tables. It was crazy that people were required to work before they could eat.

"Come on," the girl said, looking behind her and seeing that he hadn't followed her.

He thought she was going to bring the pan out for him.

Well. These people were really weird.

Still, his stomach rumbled, and he figured that if this got him food sooner, he'd oblige.

But in the meantime, he was going to ask his buddies if there was any place other than this quirky little diner where a man could get served without having to work first.

"When it's full, you just empty them into the sink. When you get a chance, you rinse them, put them on the tray, and run them through the washer." The girl showed him what to do, talking as she worked, pulling the dishes that were in the pan out as she talked, then handing the empty pan back to him.

She rinsed the rag off in the sink and showed him how to sanitize it, and then basically shooed him back out of the kitchen.

That seemed like an awful lot of information that a person needed just to clear off a table.

Maybe he was expected to carry the dishes back and take care of them after he was done eating.

But she just cleaned off that other table.

He had been to enough places in the world to know that etiquette varied from country to country, of course, even from state to state and town to town. He tried to respect the "normal" way of doing things.

As a visitor, as a newcomer, it was his job to learn the way the locals did things and fit in.

He didn't have to like it. And he didn't have to try to change things that were working just fine for everyone else.

Even if he did find this very odd.

"Thanks, kid," he said, nodding at the girl.

She was cute, with blonde hair and big blue eyes, but it wasn't really her looks that caught his gaze.

She just seemed...lonely. Or sad. He wasn't sure what it was.

But he felt like he found another hurting soul in her. Almost like a kindred spirit. Although, he certainly didn't subscribe to that kind of nonsense.

That's what his little sister would have called it—a kindred spirit.

And that's when it hit him.

That's why he felt a kinship with the little girl.

She looked just like his little sister, Mary Beth.

Man. It'd been years since he thought about Mary Beth.

He turned away, walking toward his table, but his mind was still on the sister who had died of cancer in their childhood.

They had been close, only a year apart. And he'd done everything with her.

She idolized him, and he protected her.

When she got sick, it hadn't occurred to him that she might die.

Cancer hadn't struck fear into his heart at that point, not like it did now.

He gathered the dishes off the table and used the rag to wipe it, swiping under the salt and pepper, taking time to wipe the bottles, because it annoyed him when he sat down at a table and the salt and pepper and ketchup bottles were sticky.

He wiped the seats and picked a napkin and a fork up off the floor. He wouldn't dream of leaving a table with napkins or silverware on the floor under it, but he'd always been teased as a bit of a neat freak.

Being an only child after he lost his sister probably attributed to that.

He could do things his way, and he'd gotten used to keeping things organized.

It's just the way his mind worked best.

He finished, straightening and figuring he'd take all the dishes back to the kitchen before he sat down, but he'd barely turned his back when he passed a couple with two small children who walked by. The man nodded at him and said, "Thanks, man."

Elias's stride hitched. If he wasn't mistaken, the couple just sat down at the table he cleared off.

He turned around, trying not to have an outraged look on his face.

They had. They just sat down at the table he'd cleared off.

The woman looked tired, the kids antsy, and the man, while he held humor on his face, seemed to have his hands full trying to appease the younger of the two kids.

They looked like a farming family who had worked all day, and maybe didn't have time to cook supper, and who'd come into town so they'd be able to feed their family and relax for a minute.

He didn't exactly feel bad for them, but he did feel compassion.

He hadn't done much all day. While he'd been busy researching some things on the Internet and had taken a stroll around the farm to see what his crew had been up to, he hadn't actually worked.

That was fine. He could clear off another table for himself.

So he did. Going to the other table that had been vacated and putting the plates and dishes in the pan, he carefully wiped it the same as he had the other one.

He finished with that, walking back to the cash register, going behind the counter, and taking a look over at the little girl who was back in her spot on a stool behind the counter, laughing at something one of the patrons who were sitting at the counter had said.

"I want to pay my bill," a voice behind him said.

He turned around to see an older lady waving a piece of paper in front of him.

He looked around.

"Are you talking to me?" he asked, realizing that she probably was, since he was standing on the other side of the counter.

"I sure am. I'd like to get out of here. My son's in the hospital, and I need to go visit him. But it's cheaper to eat here than it is in Rockerton."

Elias nodded, although he barely heard the woman's words.

She had mistaken him for an actual employee.

Did he really look like he was a waiter in a small-town diner?

He wore jeans and a T-shirt with a flannel over top. He didn't have an apron or hat or name tag or anything.

Still, he had noticed the waitress that he'd seen wasn't wearing anything special.

Not that he normally noticed people's clothes.

"I can show you how," a voice said at his elbow.

He looked down at the little girl.

She seemed to expect him to come behind the counter and had shown him how to do the dishes.

He had thought she was showing him as a patron, but maybe she really thought he was someone who was supposed to be helping?

It seemed to be the way everyone was acting, but he felt like he was in the twilight zone and his brain was a little slow to form the words and thoughts.

It was obvious the little diner needed help. The woman who had caught his eye when he first walked in hadn't returned, and he imagined she was probably bustling around in the back.

She looked exhausted, so whatever she was doing, he wanted to help her with it.

He wanted to shake that feeling away, but at the same time, he found himself nodding and taking the check from the woman who stood behind him and handing it over to the little girl.

She was adept at ringing the bill up, explaining to him what she was doing as she did it.

Working the cash register was simple, adding each number by hand, coming to a total, then hitting "tax."

The woman paid with a credit card. It was simple. As the transaction went through, the girl ripped off a receipt and handed it to the woman to sign.

Chapter 5

"And that's all there is to it," the little girl said to Elias with a smile. But there was still that look in her eyes, something that drew him. And maybe something more. Like her look was calculating.

But that couldn't be. She was just a sweet little girl, like his sister Mary Beth.

"Thanks," he said, wondering if she was related to the woman who had been bustling around.

Or maybe related to whoever owned the diner. That woman was probably just a manager or something who had needed to step in and help with the work since they were shorthanded.

"The order pads are right here," the little girl said, pointing to the shelves underneath the counter.

"Thanks," he said, reaching down and taking a pad along with a pen from the canister beside them.

What are you doing?

He didn't know. He wished he had a good answer for that voice in his head, but he just didn't.

It kind of looked like he was going to be a waiter for the night, though.

He told himself it had nothing to do with the woman he'd seen walking around, but he knew that was a lie.

It had a little bit to do with the girl that reminded him of Mary Beth but a lot to do with the lady that he hadn't seen again.

Maybe they'd all think the owner hired him, and it would just be an evening of him donating his time and having another glimpse of that woman. She couldn't be as compelling as what he thought she was. He was sure about that. He just had to see her again to prove that to himself.

Plus, obviously the little small-town diner needed help, and maybe it would help him integrate with the locals if they found out that he donated an evening of his time to help out.

He'd never done anything like this in his life before, not just taking a job that wasn't his, but also serving tables.

But it wasn't rocket science, and it wasn't even as complicated as flying an airplane. It was just delivering food to people and cleaning up after them.

He could do it.

The girl put her hand on his arm. "You can do it," she said, and he wondered if he'd spoken those words aloud, instead of just thought them in his head.

"Thanks. I guess I needed the encouragement."

She smiled like it was no problem, then said, "If you have any questions, you can ask me. My mom owns the diner."

"She does? All right. I'll ask you."

Interesting.

He shoved the pad in his back pocket, picked up the tub which he'd set beside the cash register, and walked back into the kitchen.

The woman was back there. Standing at the stove, spatula in one hand, a salt shaker in the other.

The person beside her, who he assumed was the cook, with his big white apron, was standing over her shoulder, looking at what she was doing.

He assumed she was either correcting something he was doing wrong or showing him how to make a new dish.

He didn't stick around to check, but he did admire the graceful curve of the woman's neck, obvious as she had her hair up in a messy bun.

He wanted to see her face again but didn't stand around waiting for her to turn.

Moving to the sink, he emptied his tub the way the little girl had shown him. Before the end of the night, he would ask her name. She hadn't said anything about the manager, and that was really who he was interested in. Maybe things would slow down, and he'd get a chance to talk to her.

Walking back out, after wringing out the rag and figuring he'd clear off a few more tables, he saw a line of people who wanted to pay. So he stopped and took care of them.

Then, he still didn't see any other waitress, and the people who first sat down at the table he cleared off still hadn't been waited on. At least, they didn't have any drinks, and it didn't look like anyone was getting them any.

So, he took his tub, set it on a table that needed to be cleaned, and walked over with a pen in his hand.

It turned out the people didn't even have menus, so he had to go back and ask the little girl where they were, except he saw them in a holder beside the cash register before he got to the little girl, so he grabbed them, feeling that they were sticky, and walked back to the table.

He wanted to wipe the menus off, but there were four other tables that were waiting to give their orders, and he seemed to be the only one who was taking them, so he did. Doing the best he could with getting them down, having seen that he would need to have the prices when he checked them out, he left room for that.

He took the orders from two more tables, and as he walked back with the pad, he wondered where to put the pages with the orders on them.

He met the woman coming out.

"Why, thank goodness you're here. Thank you for just jumping in. I'm sorry I wasn't able to greet you when you first came in, I honestly didn't recognize you. I was thinking that Lya was a woman. But I'm glad to see that you got gas money."

Gas money? He almost interrupted her. He had no idea what she was talking about. But she seemed pretty sure of herself, and she kept talking, so he didn't question her.

"But I really appreciate you picking up the slack and doing whatever was needed. It's a huge help. As you can see, we're slammed tonight."

Her words came out in a rush, like she had been trying to play catch-up all evening and wasn't able to get herself to slow down long enough to even have a conversation that was any more than words just being spit out.

She also didn't give him a chance to talk, because while he'd had a few people over the years shorten his name, they usually said Eli, not Lya.

Still, oddly, that was what Mary Beth had always called him.

When she was a baby, she hadn't been able to say his full name.

But Lya had been easy for her, and sometimes, especially after she got cancer, she called him Lion.

He liked that. It made him feel big and tough, and he already considered himself a protector, so he loved the nickname.

Mary Beth had been the only one to ever call him that.

He had discouraged anyone else from giving him a nickname. He didn't really like them. Anything short of Elias didn't sound right coming from people who hadn't made it past all of his defenses and into his heart.

But he didn't correct the woman, and she didn't give him a chance to answer.

"If you don't mind, you can keep waiting the tables, and I'll give you a hand checking out. It'll be a while before you memorize the prices, and it just slows things down. On a night like tonight when we're so busy, that's all you get done. Sherry, my other waitress, had to go home sick. She hasn't been well lately, and she just couldn't do it anymore. Someday when it's slower, you can work on learning the prices."

She laughed, a little embarrassed. "I'm sorry. I'm Jane. And I know you're Lya.

I have to be honest and say when we were texting, I thought you were a woman. But I'm not disappointed or any-thing, just surprised. I'm sorry I didn't recognize you when you walked in. I should have said something, but I didn't realize it was you. Thank you for finally showing up. You couldn't have picked a better night. And again, I really appreci-ate you just jumping in and giving me a hand. It's a huge blessing. You can't begin to know how much I appreciate this."

"You're welcome?" he said, knowing that it sounded like a question, but he couldn't help it.

Her words were all rushed and pressed together. She hadn't given him a chance to talk, and now she was spinning away, assuming that he was going to take over the waitressing duties, and do the bussing too, while she helped the cook and checked people out.

It was a good split, but there was just one problem.

He wasn't Lya. He had no idea who Lya was, and he hadn't planned on being a waiter.

"And if you have any questions, you can talk to Merritt. She knows everything and can give you a hand if you need it." The woman nodded her head at the little girl that had already helped him twice. "But she's supposed to be doing her schoolwork, so she's not supposed to be working too much."

The woman gave him a tired smile, reminded him that he could ask anything he needed to know, that she didn't mind answering questions and no one would get impatient for having to teach him something twice.

With that, she whirled away, almost running back to the kitchen.

Bemused, he stood there for just a second, until someone hollered that they'd been sitting there for fifteen minutes and hadn't gotten a menu yet, and could he bring them one.

After that, he shook his head, getting to work.

He wanted to just smile a little over the woman and her rushed words, and how frazzled she looked, but also how cute, and how there was just something about her that drew him. Something that made him want to protect her like he protected Mary Beth.

There hadn't been a woman like that ever.

In fact, he hadn't thought about Mary Beth in years.

Other than maybe a passing thought on the anniversary of her death.

He had a lot of things on his mind, a lot of things that took up his brainpower and made him forget about the things that were important.

Maybe he'd go see Mary Beth's grave. He hadn't seen that in a while. Just... Now that he was in North Dakota, he wasn't sure he wanted to make the trip the whole way back to Ohio where she was buried.

Still, being here tonight made him long to see it.

One thing blended into the next, and before he knew it, two hours had passed. It wasn't a terrible job, but his feet were tired, and he'd been hustling the whole night.

It didn't begin to compare to training camp in the Air Force, but he was definitely glad he hadn't done anything all day. If he'd come in already tired, it would have been a long night.

Still, the rush seemed to slow down, although there still weren't any empty tables. At least people weren't complaining that the service was slow, and he didn't have too many angry patrons, once he got the hang of things.

He hadn't exactly come to North Dakota to be a server in a small-town diner, but he supposed being a waiter wasn't any harder than being in the Air Force.

Chapter 6

Jane couldn't believe that Lya had finally shown up.

No. What she really couldn't believe was that Lya was a man. She wouldn't have guessed that. From his texts, she had thought that she was a teenage girl, maybe one who had finished high school, who was trying to make her own way in the world, one who was doing the least amount of work possible.

That was judgmental, and she didn't mean to be like that exactly, but just from the texts she'd sent, and the jobs that she said she'd had, and the problems that she had.

The man who had shown up, Lya, hadn't seemed like the kind of man who would ask her for money to get groceries.

Tall and dark and while not strictly handsome, he oozed confidence and authority.

Maybe that was why she hadn't thought he was Lya. Of course, lots of people stopped in to eat who she didn't know.

And she had been looking for a younger girl, one who matched the picture she had in her head of the person she thought she was texting.

Well, hopefully she wouldn't make that mistake again. It was a little embarrassing now that she thought about it. The man probably thought she was nuts. That he had to start working without her even greeting him.

She appreciated it, though. It was another thing that went against the texts she had gotten. Lya didn't seem like a self-starter.

Chapter 7

"Wow. What a night." Jane gave Elias a tired smile as he brought the last load of dishes back to the kitchen.

The cook had left fifteen minutes ago. Elias had overheard him telling Jane that he'd already worked ten minutes past his scheduled quit time.

That had made Elias a little annoyed. He would have told the guy to suck it up. Would have paid him overtime, or whatever he owed him, but there were jobs to do, and they needed to be done.

But Jane had smiled, put a hand on his arm, and thanked him for his work, apologizing for the busy night and for her throwing a new recipe into the mix on top of everything.

The cook had grumbled a little, but he seemed appeased after Jane had spoken with him and walked out smiling.

While Elias had appreciated Jane's calm demeanor and kindness, he wanted to grab the cook by the neck and drag him back in.

Surely the man could see there was still a ton of work to do and that Jane was exhausted.

The little girl that had been sitting at the counter had long since left.

Jane had disappeared for a bit, too, although he wasn't sure whether the two disappearances were related.

He had assumed that Jane was some type of manager, because he didn't figure the owner would actually work with the hired help.

But maybe things were just that much different in North Dakota.

They weren't as different as what he thought though, and he kind of laughed at himself thinking that people had to carry their own dishes.

That was ridiculous.

But when a person had travelled as much as he had, he kinda got used to cultures and their idiosyncrasies.

He would have said nothing could surprise him anymore, but he'd definitely been surprised. And he'd been duped.

By himself no less.

Regardless, the evening had gone well, and he was ready to hang up his... He hadn't gotten any apron. But if he had one, he'd hang it up.

One day as a waiter was more than enough for him.

"You're not usually that busy?" he asked as Jane took the band out of her hair and rearranged it so that most of the flyaway pieces were pulled back.

He liked those flyaway pieces, they softened the look of her face a bit and made her look slightly less exhausted.

Still, regardless of how her hair looked, there was something compelling about her face.

"No. We haven't been that busy in a long time. I'm glad. It's...not always a profitable venture."

"Owning a diner?" he asked, going a little bit out on a limb.

"Yes." She smiled but didn't seem surprised that he knew.

"Especially in a small town," he commented, just because he wasn't sure what else to say. How did he broach the subject that he wasn't who she thought he was and today was his first and last day?

"I really appreciate your help. You are a natural. Although, you've definitely been well-traveled."

His brows pushed together. How did she know that?

She didn't see the expression on his face because she had already turned to the dishes and was loading them in the washer. "We're closed tomorrow. We don't always close on Tuesdays, but I've been doing it, just because we've been so short-staffed. I need a day off. I'm not sure whether Sherry, the other waitress, is going to be able to make it back Wednesday, so if you want to, you can just plan on taking her shift. And once I talk to her, we'll get something figured out to split the time between the two of you. Normally, one waitress is enough, with the cook and me helping on both ends. But tonight...wow. I'm not complaining, but wow."

He had to smile. She sounded excited and exhausted at the same time. They weren't typically two emotions that went together.

Still, he opened his mouth to tell her that he wasn't coming in again.

She pushed her hair away from her face with the back of her wrist. "It is so hard to find help nowadays. If you hadn't shown up, we would have had a lot of angry customers. And not to burden you with my problems or anything, but I honestly feel the weight of responsibility so hard, needing to make this diner successful to provide a place for my girls. It's so hard to make ends meet as a single mom."

He paused as he wrung out the rag.

He felt like he would be really leaving her in the lurch if he told her that he wouldn't be coming back in.

Maybe he could stay until she found someone else. Or at least until Sherry was completely better.

Fifteen minutes later, all the tables were cleared off, the salt and pepper shakers had been refilled, and he'd wiped all of the menus as well.

Walking back into the kitchen, intending to help her clean up, he ran into her at the door.

"You go on home. You were initiated by fire today. Hopefully your second day won't be nearly as bad." She gave him a smile and held out her hand. "It's so nice to meet you, Lya."

"It's Elias."

"Oh. I'm sorry. I'm not sure how I shortened your name." Her brow crinkled like she was trying to remember. "Anyway, nice to meet you."

He couldn't resist her smile, although his lips just quirked, and he didn't give her a full-on grin.

Instead, he was caught by her eyes. By the exhaustion, which he wanted to help with, but also by the spirit behind them.

She was different. Different than other women that he'd talked to. Went out with. Or worked with. There was just something about her that drew him, like she was holding him on a fishing rod and reeling it in.

Part of him wanted to get away, and part of him wanted to spend more time with her.

"Where can I see the schedule?" he heard himself saying.

When had he decided he was going to come in again? Wasn't he going to tell her that he wasn't working for her? That he had no intention of being a waiter?

He hadn't really had any intention of being a rancher, though, either.

Would being a waiter be so bad?

Aside from the poor pay, which he didn't really need to worry about too much, since he shouldn't have too many expenses, he didn't mind the work. Maybe a few months of mindless serving would be good for him. He had to believe that would be true. Maybe that was just what he needed to decompress after the trauma of the last few years.

"Oh. Right. Let me show you. And Wednesday, if you don't mind coming in a few minutes early, you can fill out the forms you need to fill out. You're supposed to fill them out first, and I need to submit everything, so please don't get hurt walking out of the diner, because you're not covered under workers' comp just yet."

"I'll watch my step," he said. Since he wasn't really planning on working there—was he?—he supposed it wouldn't matter.

She took him over, showed him the wall where the schedule was, then showed him how to punch in to her simple computer system.

She gave him a few more odds and ends and grabbed a paper out of a drawer that had all of the prices and instructions on it and gave it to him to look over.

There weren't many.

She was easygoing and relaxed, and he stood there, her scent drifting up toward his nose, reminding him of energy and smiles and cozy blankets of all things.

He didn't even like blankets.

Yet, her scent made him long for one. Almost.

Regardless, he thanked her, figuring that she still had another ten minutes of work to do.

As he walked out the back door, he realized there was a set of steps that went upstairs. He thought that maybe she lived right on top of the diner.

How convenient.

He might just hang around and make sure she got up okay.

Maybe on Wednesday, he'd strike up a conversation with her. He wasn't interested in any kind of long-term relationship, but Jane seemed like the kind of woman that he'd like to be friends with.

And having friends wasn't a bad thing.

Chapter 8

"Did you hear what happened at the diner last night?" Helen asked as she sat down on June's chair.

Normally, she and her friends met at the community center, but June had been going through cancer treatments, and when she was too weak to leave her house, Helen and Miss April met there.

Her husband was seldom home, although when he was, it made things uncomfortable, since he wasn't an overly pleasant man.

He could be charming when he chose to be, but normally he didn't choose to charm June's friends.

Regardless, Helen would put up with June's husband, because she loved June. And June didn't like to hear her complain about him, so Helen closed her mouth and tried not to.

Even though she personally thought June would be better off without him.

Her own husband wasn't always the best, and she struggled in her marriage, but he wasn't neglectful and unkind the way June's husband was.

Actually, June's husband was a liar, and that was probably his biggest fault. June had caught him in many lies, and Helen suspected that if he'd lied about little things, he probably lied about big things, like being true to his wife.

Of course, she never mentioned her suspicions to June, because if June didn't know, and she was content, Helen didn't want to rock the boat.

Even though she kinda felt that maybe her friend was being too kind to her husband. Or maybe too gullible.

"I heard. And I also happen to know that Elias, that's the man's name, is single. He's the one that Gideon was talking about when he said he was a handyman."

"I heard he was tall," June said weakly from the bed.

Jane might have talked to her. Or Kathy might have been in as well. Helen wasn't exactly sure where June would have heard that, because she knew that June hadn't been out.

She wasn't supposed to be in large crowds of people, because of germs, and her husband certainly wasn't bringing any information to her.

At least not from the town. He'd been spending a lot of time at their pretty, divorced neighbor's house, helping her.

Funny that he wouldn't or couldn't do dishes for June, but he'd done pretty much anything the neighbor lady had asked him to.

It made Helen angry, and she tried not to think about it.

"I think he'll be a perfect match for Piper. We've been looking for someone for a while, and I really want to jump on this guy. It seems like single guys move into town, and they're only single for a short amount of time before someone snaps them up. I want to give Piper a chance."

Helen looked at Miss April. She seemed quite determined.

Ever since Miss Charlene had gotten married and retired from her match-making job, Miss April had slowly been taking it over.

In Helen's opinion, Miss April had great marriage advice but maybe wasn't the best matchmaker in the world.

"Do you think that that man would be interested in a woman with six kids?"

"Piper is a really fantastic woman," Miss April said, patting her hair.

"She's a great hairdresser, but I heard the man was kind of quiet, taciturn, and seemed very much like a leader. A little commanding. Almost like he was ex-military."

Usually her sources were pretty good, and that was actually a compilation of things that she'd heard from various people.

It had certainly been big news last night.

This time of year, with people retiring into their houses to escape the cold, and the only thing going on was Friday night football, the rest of the week, folks were looking for something to talk about.

Elias had provided a great distraction.

Elias and Jane. Jane hadn't mentioned to anyone that she was hiring him. In fact, Helen wanted to talk to her about that. She'd shocked the whole town.

It wasn't like Jane to keep secrets.

At least as far as Helen knew.

"I'm sure that they'd be perfect together. That's what those children need. A man who is commanding and not afraid to give orders. They need to be whipped into shape." Miss April nodded her head, like she knew all about raising children.

Helen would give her that she was excellent at marriage, but she wasn't sure about the whole child raising thing.

"All right, this is what we need to do. We're going to post a lookout, who will alert our sources. The next person who sees him in town will contact me. If you hear something, you get a hold of me right away, and I will immediately go and see if I can't grab him, and we'll get him shuffled out to Piper's house as fast as we can. Keep him there as much as we can, and you know what they say: familiarity brings marriage."

"Is that the way that saying goes?" Helen asked, squinting her face up. She didn't think that quite sounded right.

"Something like that. It's close enough." Miss April smiled.

Helen smiled back, loving the lady, even if she was a little eccentric at times.

Still, everyone could be forgiven for a few quirks in their personality. She herself certainly wasn't perfect, and she couldn't expect the people around her to be, either.

"I wouldn't be the slightest bit surprised, June, if you end up with a lot of meals from the diner in the next few weeks. I would say that people are going to be wanting an excuse to go in and see the new waiter."

The ladies laughed together, and they all nodded knowingly.

Regardless of whether Piper ended up with Elias or not, Sweet Water was going to be watching.

Chapter 9

Tuesday, Elias had planned to stay at the ranch all day. But there was a leak under the faucet in the kitchen and a light bulb in the closet upstairs that didn't work.

He had also gone down to the basement and had seen that there were several electrical projects that he could probably tackle before winter. He didn't like the almost bare wires and the patch job that had been done down there, maybe after the basement flooded. Or maybe just because it was so old. Whatever the case was, he figured a trip to the hardware store wouldn't hurt.

All right. And he kind of felt, upon waking, that all the things he was thinking about Jane were probably just a dream.

Or a figment of his imagination.

Or he was jetlagged.

He laughed at the last one, because he was not jetlagged. He hadn't flown anywhere and had only crossed one time zone, coming from eastern Ohio.

Making a list of the things he needed, he got in his Jeep and drove to town.

It wasn't quite as cold as it had been, which was a good thing, but the spots in front of the hardware store were all taken.

He parked his Jeep down the street a bit and walked back.

The diner was dark.

He wondered what Jane was doing and called himself all kinds of fools for agreeing to continue to work for her.

Except, he was actually kind of looking forward to it.

It would keep him busy, even if his personality wasn't exactly suited to be a server.

It would also help him get to know the townspeople. Most of them had been very friendly and kind last night, despite the delays and the waits.

Only a couple had been rude, and he almost guessed that they might have been out-of-towners.

A tone sounded when he walked in the hardware store, which smelled a little bit of grease and a lot of fresh-cut lumber mixed with a little lemon.

It smelled good. He'd always liked to tinker with things, which had been part of the reason he joined the Air Force to begin with.

He'd thought about becoming a mechanic, but his aptitude test had shown he had potential as a pilot and commander, and so he ended up going that route.

Still, he learned what he could, not just so that he could relate to his crew, but because he was interested in how things worked and enjoyed fixing things.

After browsing the shelves and picking up all the things on his list, he made his way to the counter.

An older gentleman, with salt-and-pepper hair and kind eyes, rang up his purchases.

"You're new in town," the man said as he put the things into a bag.

"Yep." Elias wasn't used to offering unnecessary information, and he had to remind himself that this was a small town, and people were friendly. And they expected him to be as well. "I just got in the day before yesterday. I'm...working at the diner."

The man's lips twitched. "I thought that was you. I heard there was a new hire, and he didn't look anything like an actual server." The man shook his head. "Sheila and I were going to go out to eat last night, and I talked her into staying in because it was so cold out. After I'd been in the store all day, I just wanted to sit down and relax in my own home. I should have allowed her to make me go. It would have been...interesting."

"I don't want to scare anyone away from eating at the diner, because from what I understand, the food was good."

He'd never gotten anything to eat last night. He'd meant to eat after his shift was over, but when he saw the cook had left, he'd gotten upset and hadn't even thought. Not that he would have asked Jane to make him anything after the day she'd had, but still.

He'd been hungry and ended up opening up a can of green beans when he got home and eating that.

"We were busy last night, and I'm kind of glad you didn't show up."

"Folks I talked to said you did a good job, for your first day."

"Thanks." He wanted to say that serving wasn't a hard job, but it was, actually. Hard as in there were a lot of things to juggle, people expected you to remember what drink they had, when he had served more than several hundred people several hundred different drinks, and he was supposed to remember their exact request?

He figured a few tricks in his head might help with that, but that, and re-

membering to ask about people's orders, remembering to get everything
that was on their order on the tray, and
a bunch of other things. It was definitely
a learning curve.

He could see that it would get easier
once he had a few things memorized.
Like the prices.

The few times he'd had to check someone out had been pretty difficult.

"Well, maybe the wife and I'll be heading there tomorrow. Are you going to be
working?" the man asked.

"Yes," he said without hesitation. If he
was being honest, he was looking forward to it.

The door tone sounded just as he picked up his packages, and the man said, "I'm Bob Rice, by the way."

"Elias." They shook, and Elias turned, intending to head out the door, but an older woman, he would guess she was in her sixties, strode up the aisle toward him.

"Are you Elias Stone?" the woman asked, almost sounding like she was accusing him of something.

Was she ex-military?

Of course she wasn't. She looked as civilian as a civilian could look.

Although, certain undercover civilians were very good at their job.

"Yes, ma'am?" he said, bracing himself. After the court-martial, he wasn't sure what to expect.

"I'm April Lansing. I heard you were in town, and I also heard that you were very good with handyman type things. Is that correct?"

"It is."

"I heard you had a job at the diner, but I was hoping you would have some time to do some side projects."

"I might," he said cautiously, not wanting to get into anything that he couldn't get out of. But at the same time, this was an opportunity to further integrate himself into the town and also to keep his mind off the past and set it on the future.

It looked like God was opening a lot of doors for him, and he intended to walk through all that he could.

"How did you know I do some handyman work?" he asked, knowing that sometimes gossip made the rounds in a small town faster than it might go if a person went online. But this was super-fast, considering he hadn't told anyone, and he was at the hardware store for the first time.

"Gideon told me," the woman said, like that settled it.

Elias wondered what in the world Gideon would have had to talk to this woman about him for, although he supposed he could see Gideon announcing that his friend was coming and he was a good handyman. If the lady had said that she was looking for one.

Regardless, he was busted for now.

"Would you be interested in a job?" the lady said.

"I might be," he said, again cautious.

"I have a mom, a single mom. She has a bunch of kids - six. The town always tries to do things for her, but she has some wiring that needs to be done in her house, along with an addition she needs put on, and we were hoping that you could give her a hand."

"I might be able to. Does she live in town?"

"She lives outside of it just a bit but doesn't own much property. She's a hairdresser and sells beauty products, which doesn't make her a lot of money but makes enough to survive. Barely."

"That's fine. I'm not super concerned about the money right now." It was true. He had enough of seeing people lying for greedy gain to last him a lifetime. He'd love to be able to live without money at all. He'd witnessed what people would do—sell their integrity—when faced with losing it.

He didn't want word to get out that he did things for free, but at the same time, if she was a single mom with six kids, he wouldn't mind giving her a discount. Or doing some work gratis.

"I guess you could go ahead and give her my phone number, and we can set up a time for me to go out and look at her house and see what I can come up with." He paused. "I have to do it around my job at the diner."

"Oh, I know." Miss April waved her arm in a dismissive gesture. "That won't be a problem. Everyone knows you're working for Jane. But on the side, we thought you could give this lady a hand. I know she'd appreciate it." The woman paused, and then she rushed on. "Actually, I can take you to her house right now. If you aren't doing anything else?"

He hadn't been planning on that, but he supposed it wouldn't hurt. He had the whole day ahead of him, and the projects he planned to start were basically to keep him busy. They weren't emergencies.

"Sure. I've got time." He hoped he didn't regret it.

"All right. Then we might as well go out, and I'll introduce you two. Then you guys can take it from there." Miss April looked pleased with herself, and he had the feeling that maybe there was something more to Miss April's request than just the surface idea of a single woman needing help.

He couldn't put his finger on what it was, but he also couldn't shake the idea that there was something a little deeper going on than what first met the eye.

He nodded at Mr. Rice as he left. Looking at his expression confirmed his suspicion.

He vowed to be on his guard.

Chapter 10

Toni rolled over from where she lay in bed.

She'd woken up with a sore throat that morning, and her mom had made her stay home from school.

She wasn't happy about that since she hated missing school. She always felt like there was so much to catch up on, and she never could figure out what exactly she missed.

The gaps in knowledge bothered her.

Still, her mom had said something about her droopy eyelids and told her that there was no way she was going to allow her to go to school.

Her mom knew how much she hated missing, and she had muttered more than once that it was odd that she had gotten the one child in the history of the world who didn't try to make up illnesses in order to stay home but rather hid them so she could still attend classes.

Regardless, Toni had been lying in bed since seven o'clock in the morning, and she was bored out of her mind.

It was only ten o'clock, and it would be another five hours at least before she saw her friends.

That was if their mother would let them come visit her, since she was sick.

They'd probably stand on the sidewalk and wave up to her window at her.

That was one of the benefits of living in town.

Her mom worked from home. She was some kind of virtual assistant to the CEO of a gas company.

Her hours were nine-to-five, and so she'd spent two hours with Toni before she had to go to work herself.

Even though she was just in the other room, and Toni could go talk to her if she needed to, she left her alone.

Her boss was really demanding, and Toni knew that, while her mom would stop to take care of her, she shouldn't interrupt her unless it was an emergency.

Sighing, tossing and turning, before throwing the covers back and putting her feet in her big pink bunny slippers, she padded to the window.

Maybe there'd be something to watch outside.

Perhaps Billy would be chasing Munchy again, and she could laugh as the animals ran up the sidewalk.

Or maybe Cord Stryker would be taking his Percherons for a drive and go through town.

That didn't happen often, but it was fun to watch when it did.

Or it was fun to watch the Powers family's big trucks going through town.

But the streets were quiet, except for two people on the sidewalk.

Toni almost turned away, but at the last second, she froze, her face pressing against the pane, her eyes wide.

No. It couldn't be.

Miss April couldn't possibly have her hands on their man.

That was the man who was supposed to marry Miss Jane.

As soon as they got Miss Jane matched up, then they would be free to find a husband for Toni's mom. They had agreed that since Miss Jane had two children, and Toni was an only child, Sorrell and Merritt needed a dad before she did.

It had been a bit of a sacrifice, because she didn't know how long it would take, but it was the right thing to do.

After all, if two people could find a dad, they should do that first. But this was outrageous. He'd only been in town two days. And there was Miss April, grabbing his arm and leading him down the sidewalk, surely taking him to some single woman's house, and they'd never see him again!

Hurrying over to her nightstand, tripping on the edge of her hem, catching herself in her haste, she grabbed her phone and texted Sorrell.

Miss April has our man!

Toni didn't expect an answer right away.

They were allowed to have phones in class, but if they were looking at them while the teacher was talking, they got in trouble. She couldn't wait and sent another message.

> **We've got to do something. Tonight.**

She paced the floor, wondering what she could do. She was sick. She wasn't able to do anything. Her mom would never let her go out. That was the rule. If she stayed home from school because she was sick, she didn't play that day.

Not that her mom ever had to enforce that rule with her. Since she never stayed home from school unless she was forced to. But still. There was no way she was going to be any help to her friends. But they had to do something about this. She checked her phone for what felt like the hundredth time in the last fifteen seconds, and finally a text came back.

Are you sure?

Her fingers flew over her phone as she answered her friend.

Yes! I just saw them! Just now!!!! She has him by the arm, and she's dragging him down the street!!!

She sent that message, and then waiting for a message to come back from her friend, she had to continue to write. She was so worked up she couldn't keep her fingers still.

She's going to have him matched up with someone else!!! I just know she's dragging him up to some single woman's house!!!! We were too slow!!!!!

All right. I don't know if I can get out of school or not. Probably not. But I'll try.

What are you going to do?????

I don't know.

My mom is never going to let me do anything tonight!!!!

I know. Maybe she'll let us visit.

Your mom will never let you come!

She might. If I tell her how sad you look.

Nice try! You might get a sore throat too! I really do have one!!!

I know. I know you hate to miss school. I figured you were really sick.

It hurts! And I'm tired. But I'm bored. I wish I were in school!

I know. All right, I'm gonna have to go. The teacher's looking at me. I'll do what I can. Hopefully I'll see you later.

Toni set her phone down and threw herself on her bed.

Lord, I've been praying for a father for a really long time. For me, for my friends.

Please. I know Mom says You like to give people good things. I know that's true. A dad is a good thing. Please give me one. Give one to my friends. Don't let Miss April take our man.

She sighed. Was that a selfish prayer? She wasn't sure. She decided it probably wasn't. And she tacked on an amen just for good measure.

Chapter 11

At least Miss April had allowed him to drive, Elias thought wryly as she practically jumped out of the vehicle when they arrived at the house just slightly out of town and marched up the walk, like she was in a parade.

Elias followed more slowly, something telling him that this was not going to be a visit he enjoyed.

The house was a little rundown, small, and if there truly were six kids, he wondered where they all slept.

If there was someone who needed a hand, it sure looked like this lady did.

Dried stalks of weeds stood up in the flower bed around the house, and the grass looked like it might have been mowed once that summer, around about August or something.

It made him tired just to look at the whole place.

Then the idea of six kids...

Regardless, if he had skills that this lady could use, he would happily give them to her.

He'd given his word that he'd do it already.

Miss April was already knocking on the door by the time he reached the top step and strode over to her.

There had been two other cars in the driveway, and Miss April said, "She probably has a beauty customer. She cuts hair, does perms, coloring, things like that. Foils or something that's big nowadays with the younger set."

Miss April seemed to be just making conversation, and he nodded.

"If she's working, we can come back."

Or not.

He didn't understand why he was so reluctant to be here.

He had started serving at the diner without even being asked yesterday, and now he was dragging his feet here.

It just didn't feel right.

"I'm coming," a voice called from inside.

Just a few seconds after that, the door opened, but slowly.

A kid, too young to be in school apparently but old enough to open the door, looked out through a six-inch crack in the door.

"What do you guys want?" the kid asked.

"We'd like to see your mom," Miss April said, calling the little boy by name.

"She's coming." His face scrunched up. "Are you guys going to hurt us? I'm not supposed to let anyone who's going to hurt us in."

"You know me from church."

"Sometimes people who go to church aren't very nice," the little boy said, with what Elias considered to be wisdom beyond his years.

That's what he found. People who went to church were sometimes not very nice.

The little boy stared at them, but he didn't open the door any further.

It was starting to get uncomfortable, when Elias glanced down and saw a baby, wearing nothing but a diaper, crawling around the little boy's feet.

The boy used his foot to shove the baby back, not gently, but the baby didn't cry. It was a big brother thing to do, and it made Elias smile. He tried to hide it, because he didn't want to encourage the boy.

"Dylan! Let them in!" a female voice said, sounding kinder and younger than Elias expected.

Dylan looked up at his mom and then opened the door. She had made it to the entryway and smiled apologetically.

"I'm so sorry. I have Bethany in the chair, and I just had three more curlers to put in her hair before it had to sit for a bit. I told Dylan to go see who was here, but I guess I didn't specifically say to let you in."

"It's okay. He was protecting you. He's a good kid," Elias said, nodding at Dylan.

The kid hadn't been being disobedient. He was doing what his mother had asked and protecting his family. Elias couldn't fault him.

"Well, that's a nice way to look at it," Piper said, motioning with her hand. "Come on in. You guys don't have to stand out there in the cold anymore. And we can get the door shut and stop letting the cold air in. We're not heating the outside."

Elias smiled. His parents had said that growing up too.

"I'm sorry to bother you, and if you want to go to your kitchen, we can talk in front of Bethany. There's nothing that we're going to say that she can't hear. And she'll feel less alone if we're keeping her company." Miss April bustled in the house, then stopped, waiting for Piper and Elias to catch up to her.

"It's okay, if you need to sit down, we can sit in the living room. Otherwise we can stand here. She usually takes a nap anyway."

Elias could see through the living room to the doorway of the kitchen. The back of the head of an older lady as she sat in a kitchen chair was visible from where he stood.

If Piper was trying to be a beautician and she didn't have any equipment, she was making things extra hard on herself.

But with six kids to support, she prob-ably was doing everything she could to make ends meet.

His heart went out to her, and he felt bad, but he couldn't help but contrast the way he felt for her versus the way he felt around Jane yesterday.

There had been some kind of magnetic attraction that just drew his eyes con-stantly to Jane, making him want to follow her, talk to her, just look at her if he could.

With Piper, he felt bad, but there was no attraction. At all.

She was a lot younger for one, and while she looked tired, worn out, and like she'd been working for a long time and needed a break, the same as Jane, the feelings just weren't there.

Not that he lived by his feelings. He certainly didn't.

He would be the master of his feelings and not allow them to control him.

Big words, but he knew as soon as he laid his head down on his pillow tonight, he'd have the same dreams he had last night.

Dreams of Jane.

"You said you wanted an addition put on your house. I found a handyman in town, and I know that there is a fund that the church has been raising in order to afford it. I thought I would get you two together and see if you could talk about what you needed and figure some things out."

"Oh my goodness. I couldn't accept charity." Piper's hand went to her chest, and her brows lifted, then lowered. Like she was a little offended that anyone would even offer.

"You go ahead and talk to Elias. He's got the skills to do what you need. I'm going to go on in and talk to Miss Bethany. You guys set up some times. And don't you think it's charity. It's Sweet Water coming together as a community. And someday you'll be doing the same thing and helping others. We know it. You're not slacking, you just need a little bit of a hand."

With those words, Miss April almost stomped into the kitchen.

The baby fussed to be picked up, and Dylan tugged on his mom's shirt, saying, "Mommy, mommy, mommy."

A toddler, who looked to be between the ages of Dylan and the baby that was crawling around on the floor, pushed himself on a riding toy, making all the noises that went along with it.

"I'm sorry it's so loud in here," Piper said, shrugging her shoulders, like there was nothing she could do about it.

"It's okay. There's no way you can ride one of those things and not make the noises that have to be made as you do it." He grinned at the little boy who was making the truck sound that boys seemed to be born making.

No one ever had to teach him how to make that kind of noise.

"Well, thank you." Her voice sounded a little uncertain, like no one had ever said it was okay for her kids to make excessive noise. "If you'll excuse me for just a moment." She leaned her head down and said, "Dylan. Mom is talking. Unless it's an emergency, you go play until I'm done."

Dylan didn't look very happy, but he said, "Yes, ma'am," and put his head down, walking away.

Elias didn't like the look on her face. She looked sad that she seemed to be sending her child away again. Like it happened a lot and she didn't like it.

It stirred some anger in his chest. That a man would leave his wife and six kids.

Of course, he didn't see the other three. Maybe they weren't his, maybe she had several husbands or no husbands.

All kinds of things were possible in today's day and age.

But whatever it was, there should be someone helping her.

"I'm sorry about that."

She wiped a small tear away from her eye. "The town is so good to me. I moved here with my husband ten years ago, when we had two toddlers. We had four more children, and then he was killed in a farming accident."

She sighed and looked away. Almost as though she was still sad that she lost her husband. She said that quickly and then seemed to shrug her shoulders. "I was pregnant with him at the time." She pointed to the baby who had pulled himself up on his feet and was standing, holding onto her jeans and begging to be picked up.

She scooped him up, cradled him a little bit, then blew a raspberry on his neck, making him giggle.

"I had no idea what I was going to do. But God has worked everything out so far, and I think as long as I keep working as hard as I can, He'll do nothing but bless my efforts."

She put what looked to be a forced smile on her face. Not that she was not happy, but that she was shoving away the sad parts and focusing on the happy ones.

He appreciated that type of hardworking, looking on the bright side spirit.

"I never thought I would be the kind of person who had to accept charity from the town. But they always make sure my oil tank is full and that my kids have the doctor and dentist appointments that they need." She laughed. "They even make sure I get a day off once in a while." She shook her head like she couldn't quite believe the generosity of the town.

It was one of the nicest places he'd ever stayed. He'd been in more than a few small towns, and villages overseas, and had even been stationed in Montana for a while.

Small towns had a lot of things in common, but Sweet Water seemed to be a notch above everyone else.

Maybe three notches above. He wasn't sure. Just knew he was glad he landed here. Even if he hadn't been certain of it at first.

He looked at the faded carpet, lifting his eyes to a water stain on the ceiling, then decided to be honest. "So, my ability is not really an expertise. Miss April made it sound like I can do anything, but I just tinker around. I know a little bit of plumbing, a little bit of wiring. I...don't know a whole lot about framing a whole big addition out, which is what it sounded like you needed."

"That's exactly what I need. I've got four kids sleeping in one bedroom and two more sleeping in the bedroom with me. It would be nice to have one more bedroom. And another bathroom. A bathroom would be heavenly."

"Wow. If you only have two bedrooms in here, you're in desperate need of another one."

"I am. Timothy was planning on adding one last winter before he died. As soon as the crops were in. We had some money put back, but I had to use it for the funeral. That and the hospital bill. He...lingered for a while."

Chapter 12

"That's hard."

"Yeah. It was. But at least I got to say goodbye. And he got to say goodbye to the children. He even wrote notes for them to open when they turn fifteen. All of them have one."

"That's good, I guess."

"Yeah. I didn't want him to do it, because I thought that meant he was giving up. I didn't want him to admit that he was going to die. But looking back, he was wiser than I was. And I'm glad he did."

"Yeah. Maybe he just knew."

"Maybe. But I like to think he fought until the end. He really didn't want to leave us."

"Of course not. No man wants to leave his five kids, especially when his wife is pregnant with the sixth."

"I don't think so. It was a lot of chaos, but at the end, I know he was better off leaving us. And I couldn't have asked for a better husband."

Elias nodded, not knowing what to say to that. Some men seemed to take to being a husband and father much better than others. Some men couldn't put aside their own selfishness and pride and childishness to put a wife and kids ahead of himself.

That's what it took to be a good husband and father.

He knew that much. Even if he didn't consider himself prime material to be either one.

A picture of tired but laughing blue eyes formed in his head, and he thought about them for a few moments before he pushed them aside.

No. That's not why he came to Sweet Water. Although, even after just three days in Sweet Water, he had the feeling that this was a place where he would want to put down roots.

But just because he was putting down roots didn't mean he was getting married to go along with that. And it definitely didn't mean that he was interested in being a father.

Because he wasn't.

What kid wanted to have a man who was dishonorably discharged as a dad?

For that matter, what woman would want to marry such a man?

"Well, if an addition is not in your wheelhouse, then we're wasting our time. Although, I'm glad you came out. It was nice to meet you." Piper smiled and held out her hand. It was work roughened, and chapped with calluses, although slender, like at one point it might have been a pretty hand.

It made Elias wonder why hard work made things look not pretty, while sitting around and doing nothing gave people what the world considered to be "pretty" hands.

Were they that messed up in their thinking?

Shouldn't they consider work-roughened hands, ones that were chapped, with the nails chipped and calluses thick, pretty? Those were the kind of hands that showed love. That worked hard. That had the values of hard work and integrity. Where Piper hadn't given up on life and sat around letting someone else take care of her, wondering why she got such a bum rap.

No. She dug in and got to work. Doing the best she could.

That's what her hands represented. Elias figured that the world should consider hands like hers beautiful. But especially her children should look at those hands and see the love of a mother and what she was willing to sacrifice in order to keep them fed and healthy.

He shook her hand. "One of my buddies, Gideon, is good at building. It's been a while since I talked to him about it, and I can't exactly remember what he used to do before he joined the Air Force, but I'm pretty sure his dad had a construction business, and their business was putting additions on people's houses. I could be wrong, I'll check with him again, but I know he'll be out if that's true."

"I wouldn't want to impose on him. Please don't say anything. Really, we'll be fine. I... I was actually thinking about giving the kids my room, and I'll just sleep on the couch. I don't really need a bedroom."

She wasn't saying it to sound pathetic. She was saying it as a matter of course.

"No. He'll want to come out. He loves doing it and hasn't had the opportunity for a while."

Elias wasn't entirely sure that was still true, although he did remember Gideon saying something to that effect over chow one day when they were stationed in Montana five years ago.

Officers didn't usually hang out with enlisted men, but that had been shortly after the hostage situation, which had developed a bond between them that transcended rank.

"All right. If you say so. But do me a favor, and please make sure you say that he doesn't need to feel like he has to. I just can't stand the idea that someone's coming out here and doing something that he doesn't want to do."

"All right. I'll make sure he knows that." He would also make sure that Gideon knew that the woman needed help. And if there was any way that he could possibly help her, he should. Of course, he wasn't going to tell Piper that. "He's at a convention this week. So I know it will be at least that long, and I honestly just got into town, so I'm not sure what they have planned. But even if it's not until after the first of the year, I know he'll be on it."

"The ground will be frozen solid by then. If you're going to put footers and pour cement, it's going to either have to be soon, like now, or you're going to have to wait till spring." She lifted her shoulder. "Spring might be a better date, especially if we get an early snow. Sometimes we do, but right now, the mud is so terrible it's almost impossible to work."

"All right. I'll keep that in mind. Thanks for the heads-up. I wintered in Montana, but I've never wintered on the plains like this."

"There's a big difference, when you're not in the mountains. It might not be much colder, but the wind is just terrible.

And the weather's a little different as well."

"I'll keep that in mind. I suppose I'm taking advice."

"Stock up on long underwear," she said with a grin.

He didn't have the feeling of attraction, or rightness, that he felt with Jane, but he admired Piper. Someone who could smile in the face of such hardship, a woman with spunk and spirit. He felt like this woman was probably one of the spunkiest he'd ever met and was the very definition of leading with her heart and working as hard as she could.

"I guess I'll go see if Miss April's ready to leave," he said.

The baby had put his hands on her face and tried to turn her head so that she was looking at him.

"All right. I'll follow you into the kitchen, and while you're in there, I'll get you something to drink if you want. I have coffee and water."

"I'm good."

He didn't want to hang out any longer than what he had to. He wanted to help Piper, knew she needed it, and would give her anything he had that she needed, but he didn't long to hang around her with the fierceness he felt when he'd been around Jane.

Piper was a nice lady, and he thought that she would make a good friend. But he wasn't drawn to her.

They went into the kitchen, and it was another five minutes or so while Miss April questioned them about what they'd decided.

She didn't seem very happy that he wasn't getting ready to break ground that very night.

"My buddy will do it better. Don't you want Piper to have a good addition? One that's not going to fall down as soon as the wind blows on it?"

"Well, of course, but you're here. You could do it."

"I could. Probably. But I won't do as good a job as what Gideon would. Once he's got the shell up, if he can't do the wiring and plumbing, I can do that." He lifted his shoulder. "If you haven't taken measurements, I can do that. We can figure out how much lumber we need."

"I think the guys at the church already did that. They wanted to pretty much double the size of the house and make a second floor possible."

"That's way out of my ability. You'll definitely need Gideon. I wouldn't even have an idea of how to go about doing that."

He could probably muddle his way through a small one-story addition, but he definitely wasn't going to do any kind of big job.

"That's fine," Piper said, her voice firm as she looked at Miss April. "I appreciate anything that they're going to do. And I do not want anyone to be pushed into doing something that they don't feel capable of." She softened her words with a small smile. "Since my husband died, God has provided everything we need, but I've had to be very careful not to run ahead of Him. It's tempting to do, especially with little ones. God sometimes seems so slow. But if I wait, if I trust, if I tell God I'm not going to move until I'm sure that I'm moving in His will, then He shows up for me. Every time."

It wasn't long after that that Miss April and Elias walked out, with Piper's words still ringing in his ears.

He had to wait. He had to ask God to help him. To tell God that he wasn't going to move without God's help, then God showed up every time.

Had he ever waited on God? Had he ever trusted in the Lord to do what he couldn't?

He was ashamed to say he couldn't remember any times where he'd stepped back and allowed the Lord to step forward.

He always thought of himself as a capable, take-charge kind of guy. He always forged ahead, doing what needed to be done. Deciding what he wanted and going after it.

He never allowed God to just drop something in his lap as he waited with his hands outstretched like a little child.

Maybe that's what the diner job was. God dropping something in his lap. He placed it in his path for sure, since Elias wouldn't have chosen it himself. And he almost tended to believe that it was God orchestrating it.

If that were the case, then he needed to just relax, and wait and see what God had in store for him.

Obviously, it wasn't this job, as much as Miss April wanted it to be, as she got in the passenger seat and chattered the whole way back to Sweet Water, trying to convince him that he needed to do a job that he knew he didn't have the knowledge to accomplish.

He liked the older lady, but he could see himself in her. Could see that pushing and trying and scratching and scraping when maybe the better policy was to wait.

Not that he shouldn't work hard, not that he shouldn't put his heart into everything that God placed in front of him, but just that he didn't need to try to manipulate situations, get stressed when things didn't work the way he thought they should, and try to come up with an alternate plan that would make things happen the way he wanted them to.

With that thought, he dropped Miss April off at her house, took one last glance at the dark diner, knowing he would be there before it opened the next day, and then drove home, laughing blue eyes smiling at him from the back of his mind.

Chapter 13

Did you ask your mom if you could go?

Toni looked down at the text that came in on her phone.

No. I was waiting on you.

We're ready.

I'll ask.

She took a breath, looked around the room, knowing it was as neat as it could be, and shoved her phone in her pocket, walking out.

Her mom still sat in front of her computer, even though it was six o'clock.

It was dark too, and that was another strike against Toni. That and the fact that she had been home sick all day.

"Hey, Mom," she said, coming up beside her mom's desk and leaning against it, careful not to knock anything off.

"Toni. I thought you were going to go to bed after supper?"

"I feel better."

She looked at her mom, trying to look not sick. However that looked.

Her mom took off her glasses that she only needed to use when she was working on the computer or reading a book and looked at her daughter. "Really? Your throat doesn't hurt anymore?"

"No. Just a little twinge once in a while, but not like it did this morning."

She wasn't lying. That was true. She'd slept most of the rest of the day after she texted Sorrell, and when she'd woken up, she felt a lot better.

"All right then. I guess if you don't have a fever, you can go to school tomorrow. I know how much you hate to miss."

"Thanks, Mom." She didn't move though, and her mom, who had started to turn back to her computer, swiveled back and looked at her. "There's something else?"

"Sorrell and Merritt were going to visit Miss Charlene, and I wanted to go along. Please?"

"You were home from school today. Honey, you know the rules."

"I know. But it's not like I wanted to stay home. I would have gone if you would have let me."

"I didn't want you to go out and get other children sick. And I don't want you to go out in the cold tonight and get sick again yourself."

She didn't usually argue with her mom. Whatever her mom said, she tried to do. As she got older, she realized that made her mom's burdens lighter if she didn't have to deal with Toni. To argue with her or to push her into doing what she needed to do. One of her goals in life was to make her mom's life easier.

Tonight...tonight she really needed to do this, though.

"Mom, can't I please go?" She knew she needed to have a bunch of good arguments. She should just lay it all out. But she didn't know how her mom would feel to know that she was trying to find a dad for herself. And a dad for her friends.

They'd never really talked about it. Her mom didn't know how much she longed for a dad.

"Toni, what are you trying to tell me?" her mom said, perceptive as usual.

She worked a lot, but her mom always seemed to know what she was thinking, and she always seemed to be willing to take time to talk to her when she needed to.

Toni looked away. What could she say?

She looked at the bookshelf, filled to the brim with books, with several sitting on the very top, no figurines or knick-knacks. Her mom didn't have time to mess around with things that just needed to be dusted. At least that's what she said.

She probably didn't want to mess around with a husband who just needed his laundry washed and food cooked for him.

She could hear her mom saying that, although she never had.

"Toni, talk to me. If it's something that you really need to do, you know I'll let you. You're such a good girl. I know you didn't want to stay home. You didn't ask to either. But... I want you to stay well. It's my job to take care of you."

Her mom put her hand on her shoulder and pulled her closer. Toni went willingly, leaning between her mom's knees and wrapping her arms around her, loving the feel of her mom's tender embrace.

She was ten and too big to sit on her mom's lap anymore. But she wanted to. Sometimes she just wanted to sit there and cuddle up and have someone take care of her.

Sometimes she wanted that more than anything.

Sometimes she just wanted a dad's heavy hand on her shoulder, hard and strong and capable.

Sometimes people didn't get what they wanted.

"Toni. Talk to me."

"I want a dad."

The words came out fast, and she could feel the shock that went through her mom.

Her mom pulled back, enough so that she could look Toni in the eyes.

"You want a dad?"

"Yeah. Everyone has one. I want one too."

"Just because everyone has one doesn't mean you should want one," her mom chided, and Toni dropped her gaze. She'd heard that often enough and knew that wasn't a good argument.

"A little girl needs a dad. She does. God made me to need a mom and dad." She emphasized the "and." It was true. That's what God had made, a man and wife to come together and make a family, have children, and those children needed a mom to nurture and love them and take care of them and a dad to be strong and protect them and provide for them and be the head of the home.

That's what her mom believed. That's what she was taught at church. She wanted to live it.

"What does this have to do with you going out?" her mom asked softly. Tenderly almost.

"Sorrell and Merritt need a dad too. And I'm helping them get one, then they're going to help me."

"Do I get any say in this?" her mom asked, stretching her head down so that Toni had to meet her eyes.

"Of course. You have to marry him. So you're going to have to agree."

"Maybe I don't want you picking out a husband for me."

"Maybe I don't want to not have a dad." She knew her tone sounded a little combative, and she didn't really mean it like that. But she had to win this argument. It was important.

"I didn't realize you felt that way," her mom said after a small break.

"I've always wanted a dad. Always." As soon as she was old enough to know what a dad was and to know that she didn't have one, she wanted one. "You'd be happier with a husband too. You'd have someone to help you work so you don't have to work so much. And then we could spend more time together."

She hated to play the spend more time together card, but that always made her mom feel guilty, and it usually made her a lot more compliant with Toni's requests.

It was true, but she still felt guilty.

"And how are you guys going to see Miss Charlene going to help me to get a husband and you a father?"

"I can't really say," she mumbled.

"Toni. What am I going to do with you?" her mom said, and she loved it when her mom asked that. It meant that Toni was challenging her, in a good way, and that made her feel older, and the tone of voice that her mom used always made her feel loved.

Her mom pushed her back, far enough that she could look into her eyes.

"I know I shouldn't let you. I know you should be home resting. You were just sick this morning. But..." She paused and pressed her lips together, shaking her head.

Toni held her breath.

"But you're a good kid. You never do anything wrong. And although I think we'd be better off just sitting back and letting the Lord handle whether or not you have a dad and I have a husband, I'm okay if you go see your friends."

"Really?" Toni said, jumping up and down a little. "Thank you!" She threw her arms around her mom and squeezed tight.

Her mom squeezed back. "Only for half an hour. I don't want you out any longer than that. And I want you to wear your heavy coat, your hat, your mittens—"

"Mom. I wouldn't want to go out in this weather without those things anyway. It's cold outside!"

Her mom laughed, and Toni relished the sound. Her mom worked so hard, and she just wanted to see her be happy. Not that she wasn't usually happy, but she wanted to see her together with someone, to have someone she could depend on, someone who would take care of her.

And Toni wanted little siblings.

"Thanks so much, Mom!" she said, pulling back and running two steps before she turned around. "I really appreciate it. And I'll be back in thirty minutes, no more."

"I trust you, honey," her mom said seriously, and that made Toni's chest puff out. That her mom would trust her, and say it, with that serious look that her mom had that said she meant every word.

Toni grabbed her phone out of her pocket and shot off a text to her friends, saying that she didn't have much time and she'd meet them at Miss Charlene's house.

Then she put on all the winter clothes her mom had said, plus her boots, and then ran out the door, running up the sidewalk to Miss Charlene's.

Sorrell and Merritt must have been waiting on her text. They might have even answered her, but she hadn't taken the time to look. Her phone was still tucked in her pocket.

Regardless, they were waiting at Miss Charlene's when Toni ran up. Panting.

"How did you get her to do that?" Sorrell asked, sounding astonished.

Merritt stood beside her shaking her head, her face the only thing peeking out of her high coat collar, with a scarf wrapped around her neck and a beanie cap pulled low down over her ears.

"I'll tell you some other time. I only have thirty minutes. We need to hurry."

"All right. I'll do the talking," Sorrell said, and Toni smiled to herself. Of course she was going to do the talking. She always did. She was the one who led, and Merritt and Toni were the wingmen.

Toni didn't mind at all. Maybe that's why they all got along so well together.

Regardless, she didn't have time to think about that today. She was focusing on what they needed to do. And that was get Miss Charlene to tell them what she used for the love potion when she was matchmaking.

They all walked up the steps, and Sorrell knocked on the door.

It seemed to take forever for Miss Charlene to answer, although they could hear her walking around inside.

Toni shifted from one foot to the other, tempted to dig in under her coat and sweatshirt and pull her phone out of her back pocket just to check to see how much time she had. Why did Miss Charlene have to be so slow?

The door opened slowly, and Miss Charlene stood in front of the screen door, squinting.

"Sorrell?" Her eyes lifted. "Merritt and Toni? What are you girls doing out this evening? And Toni. Didn't you stay home from school sick today? You should be in bed. I can't believe your mother's letting you run around after not going to school."

"Can we come in for a minute, please?" Sorrell asked, and Toni figured she probably knew she was being a little bit rude. You were supposed to wait until you were invited.

"Goodness, girls. Of course. It's freezing outside tonight."

Literally.

Toni figured her mom was probably right. She should have stayed in bed. Her throat was hurting a little bit after her run down the street. And she felt tired. But this was worth it. If it would get her a dad and her mom a husband, it would be so worth it.

They filed in, with Toni last.

Miss Charlene shut the door but took Toni's arm at the same time. "Does your mom know you're out here tonight?"

Toni was so glad she hadn't even considered sneaking out. "I asked her, and she told me that I could be out for thirty minutes, no more. So we have to hurry."

"Oh. All right. Well, I still might have to say something to her. If a child doesn't go to school, she certainly shouldn't be running around town after dark in this kind of cold weather especially."

"Yes, ma'am," Toni said, her eyes going down to the floor. She didn't want her mom to get in trouble with Miss Charlene. She hadn't meant for that to happen. She just wanted to meet her friends and make sure they got a hold of that man before anyone else did.

"Actually," she said quickly before Sorrell could speak. "It was an emergency. Mom knows I'm out, but she had to let me go, because it is time sensitive." She thought that she was using that phrase correctly. She'd heard adults use it and kind of thought it sounded important. Time sensitive.

"Really?" Miss Charlene said, almost looking like she didn't believe them. She crossed her arms over her chest.

"Really."

"It is. She's not lying. And she did ask her mom. She wasn't going to come, until she texted me and said her mom said yes."

Sorrell's testimony didn't seem to sway Miss Charlene's opinion at all.

Maybe Merritt figured that they had been talking about whether or not Toni got permission long enough. Because she butted in.

"We need your recipe."

Sorrell gave her little sister a dirty look and elbowed in front of her.

"My recipe?" Miss Charlene asked, ignoring the silent drama between sisters.

"From back when you were a matchmaker," Merritt said, ignoring the fact that her older sister was practically standing in front of her to get her to be quiet. "The one you used to make everyone fall in love with everyone else. We need that one. Like now."

Chapter 14

"Oh. My love potion?" Miss Charlene asked, and Toni couldn't tell what the expression on her face said.

"Yes!" Sorrell said, stepping on Merritt's toes and pushing her out of the way. "We need your love potion. The recipe, or if you have an extra batch sitting around you've already made, just in case we mess it up when we try to do it, we need it. We actually have money, and we can pay for it."

She motioned to Toni, but Toni held her hands up and shook her head.

"I think we have one dollar and seventeen cents. And we'll give you all of it, if you give us the recipe and/or any spare batches that you have sitting around."

Miss Charlene shook her head, and her eyes closed for just a moment before she opened them. "Who are you going to use this...love potion on?"

"Our moms!" Toni said, unable to believe Miss Charlene would ask such a ridiculous question. Who else did they think wanted to get married?

"Oh. Your moms. As long as you're not using it on yourselves."

"I'm only ten. I don't want to get married," Sorrell said, and she sounded like she was holding her nose and looking at a bucket full of pig slop.

"Of course not. I'm sorry. That was my mistake."

"It's okay," Sorrell said, seeming a little uncertain. Like she wanted to ask for the love potion again, but she'd already asked fifty gazillion times, and she didn't want to be rude.

"So can we have the love potion?" Toni said, unafraid. Her mom was the best mom in the entire world, and she deserved a really great husband.

She would ask for her mom.

"I'm sorry, girls. I don't know where you got the idea that I have some kind of love potion, but...I wish it were true." She laughed a little. "It would have made my job as a matchmaker a lot easier. But I just prayed and used my powers of observation."

"Your powers of observation?"

"Sure. I watched people. Whether they were single, whether they were looking, and whether they would make a good match with someone else. You can't match up someone who likes to keep the house at sixty-five degrees and gets up at four o'clock in the morning with someone who likes to keep the house at eighty degrees and gets up at noon. They are too different. They would fight constantly and never get along."

The girls stared at her. Toni wasn't sure what to think. Surely there'd be a compromise in there somewhere. She hadn't even considered the times that people got up in the morning and the temperature that they kept their thermostat on.

"Although," Miss Charlene said with a smile, the kind of smile that made Toni unsure as to whether she was being serious or not. "The most important thing you need to consider is whether their values and morals line up with each other. Other things can be worked out, truly, but you don't want to match your mom up with someone who's not a Christian, for example. And you don't want to match non-Christians with someone who feels it's really important to go to church every Sunday. They're going to fight their entire marriage. And they disagree about the most important things."

Neither Sorrell nor Merritt said anything, and Toni couldn't think of anything to say either.

They hadn't really discussed that about the man. They just needed to find a single guy. Anyone would do. Except for Paul.

"I want a man who goes to church. That's what I want for my dad to do. I want him to take us. I want to go there with a mom and dad, one holding one hand and one holding the other. Me in the middle."

Maybe it was because she was sick, or maybe it was because her friends already knew, but that was her deepest wish. To be in between her mom and her dad, holding both of their hands and walking down the street, or wherever, loved by both of them.

"If you get a dad, you might end up with some brothers and sisters. That would mean you're not in the middle anymore. In fact, you'd probably end up helping with them."

"I don't care. I'd like to. And that's okay, if I'm not between them, maybe I can just walk behind them and look at them happy together. And know I'm a part of that."

Her voice sounded wistful, but she couldn't help it. That's what she wanted.

Maybe that would talk Miss Charlene into sharing her love potion.

Did she really not have one? Toni hadn't been sure whether she was teasing them. Maybe wanting to know that they really wanted it before she would give it to them.

"Well. That's a really nice thing to think of. And I wish I could help you. But like I said, there is no love potion. It's just a matter of looking at people and their personalities and what they want and putting them together so that they can maybe see that someone that they might not have thought of would be perfect for them."

Miss Charlene looked at each of them as though wondering whether or not they would understand what she was about to say.

"Love is a lot about proximity. You can hardly fall in love with someone that you don't spend time with. And not just being in the same town. You have to be doing something with them. Working with them, working with cattle if you're on a ranch, or maybe just being in church together. In a Sunday school class or something. But more than that, you really need to pray about it. When God's ready for you to get married, He'll make sure that you meet the perfect person."

That was not what they wanted to hear. That wasn't really solving their problems at all. It was just sitting back and waiting some more. Although, it was kind of what her mom said.

"God is too slow. I'll be old and married with kids of my own before my mom finally finds a man, if I let God do it."

Sorrell took the words right out of Toni's mouth. They all agreed on that. God was way too slow.

"When God makes you wait for things, it helps you develop patience. And patience is a virtue. God wants to see that you trust Him. When you wait, you show God you trust Him. That you don't have to take matters into your own hands, but you let the Lord do it. Sometimes, it feels like He puts everything against you, just to see if you're going to continue to wait. He wants to see how big your faith is. And maybe He wants to grow it and stretch it a little bit."

"I think we've been grown and stretched enough. I'm ten. I'm not getting any younger," Sorrell said, crossing her arms.

Miss Charlene didn't get upset at them. It was one of the nice things about her. She had always been very patient with little kids. Like she understood what it was like to be a little kid herself. It was hard.

"I know. There have been a lot of times in my life where I thought God was being too slow, and I jumped the gun. I wish I wouldn't have. I almost always regret not waiting on the Lord. As I've gotten older, I've got a little bit smarter, and I know that the best things always turn out when we leave things in God's hands."

"But I'll never get a dad," Merritt said.

"You might not. But I can tell you one thing, if God wants you to have a dad, He's gonna make sure you get one. And if you don't have a dad, that's for the best. It might not seem that way. In fact, oftentimes, it doesn't. We look at our lives and we think we need this and that and the other thing to make ourselves happy and to make ourselves prosperous and to get what we want, but God looks at our lives and says, 'That's not what you need. If you get that, you'll be hurt. This is what I want you to have.'"

Miss Charlene sighed as she looked at the girls, like she wished there was another way she could tell them what she needed to say.

"I know it's hard, girls, but there seriously is no magic love potion. And while it doesn't hurt to try to reach for a goal, to work for it, it's always best to know for sure that's what God wants you to work for before you start."

"When you were matching people up, did you know that they were meant for each other?" Sorrell asked.

Toni tried to keep the surprise off her face. That seemed like a really deep question and one she hadn't thought of. But it was very relevant.

Miss Charlene looked a little taken aback, then she smiled again. "I always prayed about my matches. Always. Sometimes they didn't work out the way I thought they should, and sometimes when I was praying or reading my Bible, God would bring a thought into my mind that helped me know I was on the right track and sometimes helped me figure out what I needed to do to get two people together. So, I know you're young, but it never hurts to get into the habit of praying and reading your Bible and seeking what God wants you to do for your life. I promise you, you won't regret that."

If Miss Charlene promised, it was most likely true. Toni knew that, even if she felt dejected and extremely disappointed.

"Now, Toni. You promised your mom thirty minutes, so you better start walking home, or you're going to be late. And

I don't think you want to be running in this cold weather. You're liable to get sick again."

"Yes, ma'am," Toni said, knowing her disappointment and disillusionment was loud in her tone.

She didn't even bother to hide it.

Both Sorrell and Merritt walked out of Miss Charlene's house with slumped shoulders.

"I'm going to be calling your moms in ten minutes and making sure that you guys got home okay," Miss Charlene said before she closed the door behind them.

"Well, that didn't go as planned," Toni said, kicking a stone on the sidewalk, only to find out it had frozen to the cement. The stone didn't budge, and all she got was a stubbed toe.

"No. It didn't," Merritt said, but Sorrell was quiet.

Then, she ripped her gloves off and pulled her phone out.

"I found this today in school. During study hall," she added hastily, with a look at her little sister, and Toni figured she wanted to make sure that Merritt didn't have any reason to go home and tattle on their mom that Sorrell had been on her phone during class. "I didn't know whether we should use it or not, but considering there's no love potion, we might want to try it."

Toni stopped, and they formed a circle, with Sorrell swiping on her phone until she brought up what she wanted.

"Listen to this. 'I cooked this chicken for my husband, back when we were dating. It wasn't two days later that he proposed to me, and we were married two months later. We served this chicken at our wedding reception. It's called Marry Me Chicken.'"

"Well."

"Whoa."

"I know, right?" Sorrell said to their exclamations of amazement. "It's not a love potion, but apparently the ingredients combined in such way that it makes someone propose marriage." Her eyes got big, and she looked to the side for a moment. "I suppose there were a lot of weddings after that wedding reception."

"Do you really think it works for every-one?" Merritt asked, sounding hopeful.

"I don't know. But we can try. I thought the love potion would be better. We know it works. But if Miss Charlene is telling us that there isn't one..." Sorrell stopped. She seemed to struggle for words for a moment. "I'm not sure there isn't. I kind of feel like there is."

"She said she prayed for them to get together. Maybe that's what we should do?" Merritt suggested.

"Should we pray for them to get to-gether if we're not sure that they're sup-posed to get together? We have to fig-ure that out first, but the problem is, by the time we figure out they're meant to be together, someone else will have snatched him up."

Toni knew Sorrell was right. Although her mom always said Miss Charlene was wise and they should listen to her. Plus, when her mom and Miss Charlene said the same thing, maybe they were onto something.

So she said a little prayer.

Lord, if the Marry Me Chicken is supposed to work, please let it work.

There. Now she had pretty much put it in God's hands, but Charlene had said it was okay for them to work as hard as they could.

Now, she felt okay with jumping in with both feet.

"I have an idea, and I think this is what we should do."

Chapter 15

"**G**ood morning."

Jane startled at the unexpected voice, her hand flying to her throat.

She jerked her head up to see Elias coming in the kitchen.

"Good morning. Wow. You're early. I didn't hear you come in."

"The front door was locked, so I came around the back. I figured that at the very least, your kids had to go outside to leave for the bus, so it would be un-locked."

"Yeah. I'm sorry. I never told you that that was the door you should come in." She shook her head. "It doesn't really matter. Whatever door you come in is fine. I didn't expect you to be half an hour early."

She was regaining her equilibrium. She had been thinking about him, and then he just walked in the door.

"Looks like you're getting something ready for lunch."

"Actually, this is just a small batch of something I'm trying out. I wanted to test it and see if people would like it before I made it in a large quantity."

"I see."

"Since you're here early, maybe you can be my guinea pig?" She gave him what she hoped was an endearing smile, to try to talk him into it.

She couldn't believe that he'd actually showed up. She wasn't expecting it, honestly.

As unreliable as he sounded in his texts, she figured one day of work would be enough and he would quit.

It was funny though, since he didn't seem anything like the person he was in his texts. If she hadn't known, hadn't seen, hadn't read what kind of person he was, she would have looked at him and thought that he was dependable, reliable, and a solid man to have around.

Just went to show that looks could be deceiving.

"I'll be a guinea pig. Especially if it involves food."

"All right. It's all ready, I was actually just breaking the chicken up." She reached around and grabbed a clean spoon. "You can let me know if I need to add anything."

She scooped some of the chicken out but didn't really hold her breath as she gave him the spoon. She was pretty confident in her cooking skills, and she didn't think it was going to be terrible. She just wasn't sure what it needed to make it really good.

She used the time as an excuse to study his face. He hadn't shaved, and she liked the rugged look of the stubble on his face.

It probably kept him warmer too, but it just gave him a rough look that made her heart flutter a little.

Of course, that same look on any other man didn't make her heart flutter, so she wasn't quite sure why she was blaming the stubble for the heart fluttering that she was having a problem with.

His hair was cut short, his face serious and a bit craggy. He didn't quite look like Abraham Lincoln, but he did have a slightly larger than normal nose and prominent cheekbones.

They were more filled out, as the man wasn't thin.

But as her eyes gazed back over his face, she realized that he wasn't smiling.

In fact, he almost looked like he was going to throw up.

Oh no. That was not the reaction she was going for.

"You can spit it out in the garbage can," she said quickly.

She hadn't expected that.

Grabbing a spoon, she dipped it in while he said, "I'm sorry. That was just...about the worst thing I've ever eaten. I'm sorry. I don't mean to insult you, but I just can't think of anything nice to say right now." He spit in the garbage can again and then said, "Mind if I grab a glass of water?"

"Oh my goodness. I'm sorry. I should have offered you one. Please. Do whatever you need."

"A fire extinguisher would be great," he said, which made her think that maybe the chicken was too spicy. But she hadn't put anything on it that would make it too spicy to eat.

"Is it spicy?" she asked, sniffing it and realizing that the smell really didn't appeal to her.

"No. It's just...salty?" he finally said.

She thought back. She couldn't really remember adding the salt. Maybe she had done something weird.

Giving the spoon a careful look, she took a little bit, and a small taste was sufficient enough to tell her that batch of chicken was getting thrown away.

"I don't know what I did. I don't even remember putting salt in."

"Maybe you just weren't paying attention and dumped it in instead of measuring it out?"

"Maybe," she said, trying to think back. She'd been daydreaming while she was making it. Maybe it was her confidence that made it seem like whatever she made was going to turn out okay, if not spectacular. And she'd just been too overconfident.

It didn't really matter what she'd done. She had the spices in front of her, and nothing that she had on the counter would have done that. So it must have been too much salt. And she just hadn't realized it.

Shaking her head in her foolishness, she set about dumping the inedible food out and cleaning her pot.

"Let me give you a hand."

"You don't have to." She looked up at him. "You're not on the clock yet."

"I wasn't thinking I was. I was just going to do it because I'm here and you need help."

She smiled. "Sorry. Seems like when you run a business and someone comes and gives you a hand, they want to be paid for everything."

"Well, not me. Although, I don't turn money down."

"Me either," she laughed.

She handed him the pot and he took it to the sink to scrub it out while she put the ingredients away and prepped the kitchen to get ready for the noon rush. Wednesdays were the only days that they opened late. That way she had a day and a half off, ostensibly.

Normally, she was trying new recipes, or doing deep cleaning, or washing windows, or doing something that would help her business succeed.

Still, she considered it fun, and it was a break from the cooking and the waitressing and the checking out that she normally did when the diner was open.

"There aren't too many places to get desserts around here?" he said with his back toward her.

She didn't want to look over. She already had trouble admiring him too much, and although she didn't want to admit it to anyone, and particularly not to him, he was almost certainly the reason that that batch of chicken hadn't turned out.

She'd been thinking about him.

She didn't have time to think about men. She really hadn't had that problem before Monday, either, and she wasn't sure what to do about it.

It didn't help that he was working with her.

Although, from his track record, that wasn't going to last long.

"I used to serve more, and the lady who owned the diner before me served a lot. But we don't sell too many, and they have a tendency to get old. Plus, the used bookstore down the street has really gotten into the baking business, and if people ask, I always send them down there."

"I see."

He had asked her a question, so she figured it was only fair that she got to ask a question.

So she asked the one that had been on her mind.

"What are you doing in Sweet Water?"

It was a small town with not much opportunity, and people didn't typically just come. It wasn't like it was a top relocation spot for yuppies or anything.

"My crew is here. They moved onto the Sweet Briar Ranch a while ago. I bought a fifth of it with them, but I thought of it as a business investment. I hadn't thought I'd be living there."

"Oh? What were you doing that made you think that you weren't going to be living there?" she asked, thinking her question was rather casual, but he clammed up.

"Nothing. I don't talk about it."

Well, that kind of put her in her place.

"I'm sorry. I was prying. Small towns." She could use the small-town excuse, but she herself was curious about him. Wanted to know everything there was to know.

"No. I was the one who was rude." He dumped the water out of the pot and set it on the counter. He turned around and looked at her, leaning against the counter and crossing his arms over his chest. "I was in the Air Force. And when I got out, I was a little...lost."

"I've heard of that. You get out, and nobody's telling you what to do anymore. So you have to live life for yourself again, and one of the purposes of the military is to make you not want to live life for yourself. So, you kinda have to recondition yourself to society."

"That's exactly right." He eyed her like he wasn't expecting her to understand.

"I wouldn't know that on my own. We just have a lot of airmen who come through. And a lot of men from Sweet Water have served in the armed forces. Not necessarily the Air Force."

"Because of the base in Montana?"

"Yeah."

She didn't know anything more about it than that.

"So you love the Air Force?" she asked, wiping up the area where she had been working.

"You could say that. I planned to make a career out of it."

He seemed surprised he said that. She caught his look because she'd jerked her head up. He had said that he had left the Air Force. People who plan to make a career of it don't leave it.

"What happened?" She narrowed her eyes.

He paused, almost as though he wanted to say "I don't want to talk about it," when he had already said that and then apologized for saying it. "I was court-martialed. And they found me guilty. I was dishonorably discharged."

Her brows lifted. Going way up. To her hairline and beyond, it felt like.

Maybe they were hanging out on the ceiling somewhere.

"You don't strike me as someone who would be dishonorably discharged from anything."

But then she thought about his text. How he'd gone from job to job to job.

"When did this happen?" she asked.

"I've been out for a year."

"I see. That must be why you had so many different jobs you were texting me about."

"Wait, what?" He sounded like he had totally missed the gist of their conversation, and so she repeated herself.

"You went from being a masseuse to a tattoo artist, and a couple other things."

"I don't...." He drew his brows down. "I've never been a masseuse."

"In the texts that you were sending me." She couldn't believe he was acting like he couldn't remember texting her. She wanted to call him out. She held her tongue but grabbed her phone out of her pocket.

She swiped and clicked, glancing up at him and seeing that he looked curious. Like he really wasn't sure what she was going to show him.

That's when the first premonition hit that maybe she'd just made a very big mistake.

Her fingers slowed down.

Maybe he didn't look like Lya, didn't look like someone who flitted from job to job and who would text and ask for gas money, who wouldn't show up for work, who would promise to come in then not make it and not text her to let her know... Maybe he didn't look like that because...he wasn't.

By the time she thought that, she'd gotten her texting app up and pulled up the texts, her fingers going slower and slower as she pulled them up, until it filled up her screen, and then she turned it slowly around and showed it to him.

He looked at the phone in her hand, scrunched his nose up a little, and then he said, "There's a heart emoji on the phone?"

For some odd reason, she wanted to laugh. Really wanted to laugh.

But she pressed her lips together, pulling back a little and trying to contain her embarrassment. "This isn't you, is it?"

He shook his head. "Nope."

He did not need to say anything more.

She'd never been quite that embarrassed in her entire life. But she pulled her chin up, turned her phone off, and set it on the counter.

"So... Why didn't you say something on Monday?" she asked slowly. Why would he have allowed this to happen? "You were...working when I saw you."

"No. The first time you saw me, I was coming in to sit down to eat."

"But the next time, you were working. How did that..."

She just didn't get it.

"There were a bunch of tables that needed to be cleared off and people who came in after me, and you looked overworked and frazzled."

She hurt at that. She was overworked and frazzled. It wasn't exactly a compliment to know that that's exactly how she looked.

She tried not to be insulted by it. He was just being honest. The same way he'd been about the food that was terrible. If there wasn't anything nice to say about the food, she didn't want him to lie about it. And she was glad he hadn't. It made her feel like he was an honest man, rather than someone who was just going to give her platitudes to make her feel good about herself, or to make her like him, or whatever the reason was that people said things to other people that they didn't mean.

"The person who cleared off a table had just walked by with the tub and the rag, and I figured I could just go ahead and clear another off myself, but then once I did that, people sat down at the table I'd cleared for myself."

She laughed, but it wasn't really because she thought it was funny. It was more because she was so embarrassed she didn't know what else to do.

"So you cleared off another table?" she supplied for him.

He nodded. "Yeah."

"And then someone sat at that one, too?"

"Well…I think maybe someone asked me to do their check while I was carrying the pan of dirty dishes back. And then your daughter who was sitting on the stool was super helpful and showed me how to do it. Apparently you guys were expecting someone to start work?"

His brows were raised.

"Someone you've never seen before," he clarified.

"Yeah. Lya." She pointed to her phone, sheepish.

To her surprise, he looked between her and her phone and back to her, then laughed.

"I don't know whether to be insulted or think it's funny that you think that I would use unicorn and rainbow emojis, and hearts. I didn't even know there were hearts."

"I really didn't think you look like the person that I'd been texting, but looks can be deceiving at times."

"I'll agree with that. They can. But that's kind of making the deceiving part downright outrageous."

She laughed, and he joined her, again to her surprise.

He didn't seem like a man who laughed a lot, and even if he was laughing at her, it made her happy that he was laughing.

"I don't think I've ever been this embarrassed in my life before. I am so very sorry that I coerced you so forcefully into working. And I even put you on the schedule for today. Why didn't you tell me at the end of the day that you were done?"

"I couldn't really get a word in edgewise," he said, shrugging apologetically. "I was going to, but you kept going on and you seemed so grateful, and it was obvious that you needed help, and to be honest, I really don't have anything else to do. I—" He paused like he wasn't sure whether he was going to talk, then he plunged ahead. "I told you that I was dishonorably discharged. It's not something I want to hide from the town. Even though it's not something I'm exactly proud of. But I don't really have a place to go, anything to do. So, this seemed like a good place to help out."

"I have the feeling that if you were dishonorably discharged, there was a reason for it," she said.

"I appreciate that you barely even know me, and you would say that. Whether it's true or not, there were so many people who didn't know me and didn't believe me." He paused again, and then he went on. "And there were people who knew me and knew that I could probably say something that would turn the tables at the trial, and they encouraged me to do that. They didn't understand that I had to keep my word first. Even if it meant losing everything that I'd worked for my entire adult life."

She jerked her head up. Accepting his words, even while she was surprised.

"So you could have changed the outcome of the trial by presenting new evidence, but you chose not to, because you...?" She trailed off, wondering if he would fill in the blanks for her.

"Yeah. Because I made a promise to someone I wouldn't. And when I make promises, they mean something."

She believed him when he said that. It was obvious he lived it. He had suffered because he wanted to keep his word.

"There aren't a whole lot of people like that in the world today," she said, and she couldn't keep the admiration out of her voice. She didn't want to come off as a simpering female who was groveling at his feet, but she wanted him to know she appreciated a man who thought it was important to do what he said he was going to do.

He shrugged like it wasn't important. Although, the pain it had caused him was unquestionable.

"You lost your career in the Air Force because of that?"

"Yeah. And I try not to think about it, otherwise I'll get bitter, because I wasn't joking. It was something that I had worked for my whole life, and my entire career was flushed down the toilet. When I got out, I was reeling."

He grinned, one side of his mouth twisting up. "Not quite as bad as going to prison, but I lived with my mom and stepdad while I worked on figuring out what to do. Their marriage wasn't very solid, and me being with them just made it worse."

"Yeah. That's so uncomfortable."

"I'll say. So, I'd already put the money down to buy the farm with my crew. That was before everything went down with the court-martial and the trial and everything. So, I didn't realize I wasn't going to be set for life. But I hadn't been planning on living in North Dakota. It's pretty desolate up here."

"And cold. Don't forget cold."

"True. Cold." That made him smile, then he looked around. "Why are you here?"

That was him turning the tables on her. It was one thing to talk about someone else's life. She didn't really want to talk about hers.

"I had the opportunity to buy the diner. I've always been good at cooking, and I worked at every job you can possibly work at in a restaurant, so I thought I might be a good fit. It was...a bigger job than I thought it would be, but I wanted to be in a small town because of my girls. That's what I'm working toward, being secure for them. I don't want them to have to deal with losing a home or losing anything else."

"Your husband died?"

She wasn't expecting him to ask about that. She had skirted that very nicely and thought that he would have taken a hint.

But he hadn't. Which, in his defense, she had been just as nosy into his background.

"No. He divorced me when they were little."

That was all she needed to say about that. It hadn't been her choice, although her marriage hadn't been happy. And the divorce was almost a relief, although it was also a scary thing too. Everything that she had been building in her life collapsed around her.

"I hadn't been building things quite as long as you had, but it was a collapse nonetheless. Then I had to pick up the pieces and figure out what I was going to do."

"How long ago was that?"

"Six years."

He jerked his head up, acknowledging that it had been a while. "Then you didn't come out here right away?"

"No. It took a little while, I wanted to go somewhere, but I needed to have the funds. So I stashed away what I could. A single mom with two girls doesn't usually have a lot of extra money, and that's how I landed in North Dakota. This wasn't super expensive to buy. Not like a diner would be in a town where you might actually have a lot of patrons and be profitable. But it was a step." She shrugged. "It might be the step I land on for the rest of my life, because my girls love it here. They have good friends, and I love it. Because it's a small town, one of those where everyone knows everyone else and everyone looks out for everyone. So, I will never have a whole lot of money, but I'll have a sense of community. And that's more important to me."

He nodded his head, as though he understood, and she figured he really did, after what he'd been through.

She finished cleaning up, and he finished doing the few dishes left in the sink, and they ended up facing each other, her leaning against the island in the middle of the kitchen and him leaning against the back of the sink.

She realized they'd been talking for a long time when the door rattled out front, and she saw it was people who wanted to come in.

"Oh goodness. I didn't realize it was time to open already. Time flew!" she said, looking around the kitchen, realizing she wasn't nearly as ready as she wanted to be. "I apologize again. I... I'll call Sherry and see if she's able to come in. And I'm so sorry that I coerced you into working. You don't have to stay," she said, even though she really wanted him to. There was something about him. Something compelling. Something honorable. It was not common anymore that a person met a man so willing to stand up for his convictions. Willing to go to jail for them. Willing to lose everything he'd worked for all his life just to keep his beliefs.

"Unless you have a problem with it, since I don't have any experience, I want to keep the job."

She knew she looked surprised when she glanced at him, on her way to open the door.

"Are you sure?" she asked, not wanting him to stay out of pity, but because he truly wanted to.

"I told you, I'm not doing anything else, so I might as well."

That was not what she wanted to hear. But she nodded anyway, not quite as happy as she had been earlier. In fact, a lot of the joy had dimmed at his words.

She knew she needed to focus and just be happy that she had an employee who was dependable and not worry about why he was there or that it wasn't for the reason she wanted it to be.

Chapter 16

Elias couldn't believe he'd told Jane so much of his life story.

But talking to her felt natural. And she'd been so cute when she was so embarrassed. Her face got all red. Even the tips of her ears had turned pink.

It had made him want to pull her toward him, and tuck her under his chin, and hold her tight.

It was an odd feeling and not one he could remember feeling before.

It was so comfortable to be with her, although he knew it wasn't something that he should be okay with. He should fight that feeling. He didn't know her.

Except, she had been reluctant to divulge her past as well. And yet she'd done it.

He wasn't sure if she told everyone everything, or if he was indeed a little bit special.

He wanted to believe that he was. Even though there wasn't any future for them.

He wasn't interested in getting married, and she was obviously too busy. Too busy trying to get the diner to turn a profit.

He loved that she was willing to go to a place where she doubted she'd be much above the poverty line for her entire life, but the trade-off for her was worth it because of the sense of community she would have. It was not the same as what he had done, sacrificing everything to keep his word, but it was similar. She could be so much more, but she'd chosen to be enough. To give her daughters the good things and not the expensive things. To pay attention to what mattered in life and not strive to have things that didn't matter.

So many people didn't understand that concept, and he was impressed that Jane not only understood it but lived it.

Sherry came in when she was supposed to, and it wasn't nearly as busy as it was when he had been there the day before. As much as he didn't want to, when his shift ended and it was time for him to leave, he clocked out and left.

Funny, it wasn't necessarily that he loved being a waiter so much, although he did not mind it.

It was that being with Jane made the job interesting. Interesting in a way that made him want to be better. To look good to her. And not in a way that he wanted to show off, but in a way that was deeper. Because she was deep.

He liked that about her.

For the first time in a long time, he whistled as he walked down the steps and over to his Jeep.

Chapter 17

Elias sat in the living room, his stocking feet propped up, a book open in front of him, when he heard a motor and assumed his friends were back.

They'd been texting him since they'd been gone, but they hadn't really chatted.

In other words, he hadn't told them that he'd gotten a job.

"So what's this about you working at the diner?" Gideon said before he barely had the door open.

He finished walking in, and Jonah followed behind him, smirking and looking confused at the same time.

It wasn't his best look.

"I suppose you guys want me to pull my weight around here. I'm going to have to help buy groceries at least. I needed a job. I assume you guys aren't eating any less than you used to. Which, if I recall correctly, was quite a lot."

He didn't bother getting up from the couch, and he was glad he didn't, because the guys came over, Gideon sitting in the chair and Jonah sitting on the opposite end of the couch.

They all put their feet up on the coffee table.

"So how did the convention go? I wasn't sure from your texts whether it was good or bad."

"Busy," Jonah said with a grin.

"We got a lot of leads. No one actually signed a contract, but that wasn't really the goal, although I did take my iPad along just in case anyone wanted to."

"By a lot of leads, what's that look like?"

"Well, if they all contact us, there's no way we could do it all. So that's good, but so far, the phone hasn't exactly been ringing off the hook, so I really don't know."

"I see. Well, you at least talked to people. And they're starting to get familiar with you."

"Yeah. And we have another convention coming up and then two more in January and a couple in February. We figured we would travel and go to them all, spread a wide net, get everything we can get to keep our plane busy, and if the helicopter deal goes through, we'll have an even wider range, because we can haul it on the truck pretty easily. So, we want to get all our bases covered. Make as much as we can next year, because we're going to have some expenditures."

Elias listened, thinking that their business sense was pretty good, but he really didn't know anything about crop dusting. He hadn't studied up on it, and he had to admit that he wasn't really interested. It wasn't that he didn't care, it was just that it wasn't something that interested him.

"Tell us about your job," Gideon said, after he'd been quiet for all of a half second.

"I told you, I needed to do something to earn money."

"You could work with us."

"I know. You guys seem like you're doing pretty well, and I don't know, I guess I'll do it if I need to, but I think I'm happy where I'm at."

He had to admit he was surprised at that admission. Although it was true. He really was happy with what he was doing.

"You're a...waiter," Jonah said, enunciating the word "waiter" so that it almost had three syllables. Very school-marmish.

"And you look down on waiters for what reason?" Elias asked, raising his brows.

"We don't look down on waiters," Jonah said, irritation in his voice this time.

"Then what are you trying to say?"

"That...you were an officer in the Air Force. You have the potential to do a lot more. You've got skills and knowledge and things that you bring to the table that no one else can. And...you're a waiter?"

"I was dishonorably discharged. That's going to be something that every potential employer sees. So, my supposed assets aren't nearly as great as what you're saying they are."

"You're letting that loom over you too hard. Civilians don't care about that."

"Employers will." He knew he was right.

"Apparently you can get a job as a waiter with a dishonorable discharge on your record."

"Exactly. That's my point."

He didn't want to admit that he hadn't been planning on getting a job like that. He had been planning to reach a little higher, if that's what it was. Just do something that was a little more suited to his talents, even if that was hiring on as a contractor. He didn't have his journeyman's license, but he might have been interested in getting it.

Both of his friends were looking at him like he was holding something back.

Maybe he was. His interest in the proprietor of the diner where he worked.

Jane.

Just thinking her name made him smile.

"What's that grin about?" Gideon asked, suspicion in his voice.

"What grin?" Elias said, making sure there was no grin on his face when he asked that.

He had to be careful. He didn't realize that Gideon was so astute. Or maybe it was him who didn't realize how silly his grin was.

He just knew he needed to be careful. He definitely didn't want Jane to hear that he might be a little bit infatuated with her.

Not a lot, just a little.

As in, he thought about her all the time, couldn't wait to get to work, and basically wanted to do everything he did alongside of her, including breathe.

"The grin that says that you're thinking about a girl," Gideon said, smirking.

Was that the grin that he had?

Then, he decided to pull Gideon's bluff and say, "Oh yeah. I'm thinking about a hundred girls. That's the grin I always use when I'm thinking about all hundred of the girls I always think about."

He didn't smile when he was saying it, very serious, and Gideon shrugged and looked away.

That's what he thought.

After that, they talked more about the ranch and the things the guys were planning, and how he could help when he wasn't at work. And then he remembered that he was supposed to ask Gideon something.

"I forgot, but one of the ladies in town took me out to a young woman's house who is a single mom. Her husband passed away not long ago, and she's been trying to make ends meet. She's living in a tiny house, and she needs an addition. I can do some plumbing and wiring, but I figured the whole addition thing was more of your skill set. Isn't that what you used to do?"

"Yeah. My dad owned a business where the bulk of our work was putting additions on people's houses. I can do that in my sleep."

"Well, she's interested. If you think you're going to have time."

"You better hurry, ground's going to be frozen, and you're not getting any footers in," Jonah said seriously.

"I know," Gideon said. He looked back at Elias. "They might need to wait till spring now. I could probably break through the ground, but I would need some equipment. If I'm going to do it by hand, I don't know that it's something I can attempt."

"I told her as much, but I can give you her number and you can let her know."

Elias pulled his phone out and saw there was a text from Jane.

He hadn't noticed, since he had his phone set to vibrate.

Just wanted to let you know that your check will be ready tomorrow. I forgot to tell you that the pay period ends on Thursday, and I try to have checks ready to pick up the next day. It's not normal, and sometimes Fridays are busy, so I didn't want to forget to tell you.

He grinned. She texted in paragraphs. He had more of a tendency to text in single words or even half words, abbreviations if he could.

"Must be a girl. He's got his girl smile on again," Gideon teased.

"It's a hundred girls. He told you."

He tried to wipe the smile off his face while he dug through his phone, grabbing the number that he needed for Gideon and sending it to him.

"There. Now we can watch you with your girl smile."

He wasn't going to tell Gideon she had six kids. She seemed like a nice lady, but Gideon would probably run in the other direction, maybe not even go to her house, if he knew that there were six kids involved.

Elias had to remind himself that he'd only seen three of the six when he was there. That had seemed like more than enough. He couldn't imagine adding three more to the mix.

He typed one letter and hit send, careful to keep the smile off his face so that Jonah and Gideon wouldn't laugh at him.

He couldn't wait until tomorrow.

Chapter 18

Jane blew out a breath as she descended the stairs in the predawn darkness.

She really didn't mind getting up early. But she didn't like to get up early and be cold.

Once she got into the diner and turned the heat on, things would get toasty pretty quick. That was one nice thing about a small space.

And once patrons started coming in, things would warm up even faster.

She'd be hot by nine o'clock, but for now, she shivered.

The shadow in the door didn't surprise her. And as she reached the bottom step, she walked forward, opening the door and letting Elias in.

"Your shift doesn't start until seven," she said, smiling as she opened the door for him. "And I really need to get you a key."

"So you know when my shift starts?" Elias said, grinning, and she felt like he'd almost gotten used to smiling at her and teasing her a little.

He had been so serious when he'd first come, but he'd loosened up. It hadn't taken a super long time.

"I have three employees, including myself, and I make the schedule, so yes. I know when your shift starts."

"I'll take that key," Elias said. "I can turn the heat on and warm things up for you so your teeth aren't chattering when you come down the stairs in the morning."

"I think I might take you up on that. I'll get you a key today in that case."

They laughed as they walked down the short hallway and into the kitchen. She turned the lights on, and he followed her in.

"I can't believe your girls get themselves up," he said as she started her daily routine. He'd only seen her do it for a few days, but he had figured it out and fell into step beside her, giving her a hand when she needed it.

"I wouldn't have done it when I was their age, but they're pretty responsible." She paused with a pan in the air. "I don't like it. I wish it were different, but I guess me being a single mom made them kind of have to grow up a little faster. Plus, I text them to make sure they're up. And I'm right downstairs."

"I know. You're a pretty good mom. You walk them out to the bus stop. Every day."

"I enjoy doing that. I assume someday soon they're not going to want me to do it anymore, and I'll be sad. They're old enough that I don't have to do it now, but it's just that little bit of time I get to spend with them before they leave for the day, you know?"

"Yeah. Those are the things I'm talking about. The things you make time for," he said as he put a little butter in the skillet. She always made eggs or an omelet or something for the girls to eat when they came down.

"Really? You're going to cook?" she said, bending over and pulling a box out from one of the shelves to get some supplies for the day.

"You think I can't?" he asked, pretending to be offended.

"Not at all. Go ahead. I'll watch."

"You do that. Although, I've heard that your cooking class is quite instructive, and I've been encouraged to attend."

"Really?" she asked, grinning.

"Really. So, I decided Sunday I was going to go ahead and come. See what it's all about."

"Wow. I would think you'd want to get away from this place after working here all week."

"You don't get away."

"No. But I love it. It's… It's what I do. You…you don't have to. You have the freedom to do whatever you want."

"And I want to go to cooking class." He grinned over his shoulder at her while he cracked an egg into the skillet.

"I used to have it every Sunday, but that was just too much, so now I just have it one Sunday a month."

"That's probably smart. I've heard that there's just three fellows who come. And they're starting a TikTok channel? And need to learn to cook for it? I'm not sure exactly why, or what TikTok has to do with cooking, but that's what I heard any-way."

"That's pretty much right. They come, and sometimes I have a straggler or two."

"You'll have at least one straggler this week," he said, and she grinned at him.

It was funny how he could always make her smile.

"Did you ever consider filming your cooking class and posting it online as a course or something?"

"Oh my goodness. No. I don't get that involved in it. And there are videos all over the place about cooking. If people want to learn, they can find them. So it's not like anyone would pay to see mine."

"Well, you do have the three old coots, and they're pretty entertaining. That would make it different than every other cooking show on the Internet."

"That's a good point, but they're already looking for someone. They've gotten my girls and their friend Toni to help, and they posted a video to try to get someone. It's gone viral, but they're trying to figure out how to translate a viral video into finding someone to actually come here and help them. A lot of the people who like the video live in, like, North Carolina or Washington. And they're not going to travel the distance to get here. And they're certainly not moving to North Dakota. Some of them live overseas as well."

"I see. Trying to find someone to do their channel with them has been a struggle, then?"

"Yes. They'll listen to my girls, and they're doing a little better, but I have to admire them for even trying. They're a lot of fun, and they don't sit around complaining like so many old men do, you know?"

"I don't think she was insulting me."

She grinned. "Well, if you consider yourself an old man, and you sit around and complain, take it how it is."

"She was insulting me."

They laughed, just as Sorrell and Merritt came down the steps.

"Good morning, girls, did you get everything gathered up okay?"

There had been some homework out on the table when she walked down.

"I got it," Merritt said cheerfully.

She was the morning girl. Sorrell didn't typically wake up until about dinner-time.

Jane could only figure that the classes she had before noon were the ones she got Bs in and her As came from instruction in the afternoon.

Unfortunately, most teachers did math class first, and so Sorrell had decided she wasn't good at math, since she could never get anything higher than a B in it.

Checking the time, Jane went to the door and flipped the sign over.

There was no one waiting outside. Sometimes, there was. Especially since

Elias had come. When they started talking in the kitchen, sometimes she forgot what she was doing, and time got away from her.

Twice now, she'd been late opening, for the first time since she opened the diner.

She wasn't sure exactly what that said. She was pretty certain that she didn't need to spend less time with Elias, but maybe she just needed to enjoy his company less.

Whatever it was.

It wasn't long until the cook came and patrons began coming in.

She walked the girls out to the bus and then hurried back. It'd been such a busy morning.

There was food on plates that needed to be delivered, and she could see Elias out front bussing tables, so she loaded up the big tray with four orders on it, all for one table, and hurried out.

She wasn't sure quite what she was looking at, but as she pushed the door to the kitchen open, she wasn't watching where she was going, and she ran smack into Elias.

The tray tipped in her direction, spilling everything all over her, and as she grabbed it, she headbutted him, the pain reverberating down her spine and her elbows and causing a lump to form in her stomach and tears to wall up behind her closed eyelids.

It was all her fault.

"I'm so sorry," she said, bending down to pick the stuff up.

"Don't worry about it. You go back and take care of cooking these orders. I'll take care of this mess."

"Are you sure?" she asked, standing up even as she was speaking and starting to walk away.

"I'm sure. That'll be the best and quickest."

"Thank you."

She appreciated the fact that he could assess the situation and figure out the best thing to do, even though he hadn't been working there that long.

She got a second skillet out to get hot and was able to get the order up in half the time.

This time, when she carried it out, she was a lot more careful.

The floor had been completely cleaned, although the dirty dishes still sat on the tray on a shelf and Elias was at the cash register checking someone out.

"Thanks for bringing that out," he said as she walked by him.

"Thanks for cleaning up that mess," she said, impressed that he had not just gotten the dishes gathered up but had cleaned all the food off the floor as well. And he'd done it fast.

She apologized to the table where she delivered the food. They laughed and said not to worry about it. They had seen what happened, because it wasn't like the diner wasn't all open, plus, the noise would have alerted anyone.

Regardless, it shook her, and she felt a little on edge the rest of the morning.

The rush slowed down around ten o'clock, and she had a chance to sit on a stool in the kitchen.

The cook had taken the opportunity to use the restroom, and Sherry hadn't come in.

"You still look a little agitated. You gotta shake it," Elias said, coming over to her.

"I know. I hate it when I do stuff like that though. It's hard not to castigate myself or just be frustrated, you know?"

He put his hand on her arm, and her eyes opened wide.

Thankfully he couldn't see it, because she had been looking at the counter.

She hadn't expected the jolt that went through her at his touch. Hadn't expected that one touch would make her want to lean into him, put her arm around him, lay her head on his chest, and hold on tight.

Couldn't believe she even wanted to do that. Didn't know where that thought had come from.

Then his other hand settled on her other arm, warm and firm and confident.

"Look up."

She obeyed, reluctantly, because now not only did she feel bad about what happened, she had all these weird emotions that she wasn't ready for, and didn't know what to do with, rolling around in her chest.

"What?" she asked, trying to smile.

"It's okay. Everyone makes mistakes. And as mistakes go, that one wasn't too bad. You could have spilled it all over their table."

"I have tripped as I've been delivering food, but never with four orders on a tray like that."

"It's okay. When you mess up, I guarantee you that someone is looking at you thinking, 'since she did that, it must be okay that I messed up too.'"

"Do you really think so?" she asked, grinning, because it sounded kinda silly.

"I know it. That's what I think when I see someone mess up. Then I'm glad I'm not the only one."

She looked up, caught his eyes, feeling some of the irritation and most of the guilt and annoyance at herself fading away. She smiled.

"That's what I wanted to see. That smile. I wanted a little happiness. And to see that guilt go away."

"Thanks for the pep talk. I hadn't realized I needed it."

"Hey. Anytime. That's what friends are for."

"We're friends?" she asked, because she felt like they were, but she hadn't been entirely sure.

Actually, she felt like she wanted to be more than friends, which made her feel like maybe they shouldn't be friends at all.

"Definitely. I thought we were. Did you not?"

"I did. I do. And you're right. I guess I need to repay the favor."

"I'm repaying the favor that you did for me, when you strong-armed me into working for you, without my consent, and giving me no choice."

"That was a favor?" She grinned at his teasing tone.

But his face sobered. "I think it was. I'm feeling like it was. I wouldn't have taken the job myself, and in fact, even though you pretty much strong-armed me into it, I wasn't sure I wanted it. But I like it here. I...like you."

His words made her stomach feel like Jell-O and her knees weak.

He still had a hold of her arms. Her hand started to move, wanting to put it on his waist. To touch him. To...she didn't even know.

"Is everything okay?" the cook said as he came back in.

She felt like she came back to reality with his question. Even though she was pretty sure she hadn't gone anywhere to begin with.

"Everything's just fine," she said, forcing a smile onto her face and looking back up into Elias's eyes.

Maybe they were a little more guard-ed than they had been. The tender look that had scrambled her brain was most-ly gone.

There was still concern on his face though.

"Is it?" Elias asked her. Like he hadn't just told her that he…liked her.

She wasn't sure exactly what that meant, but she definitely liked him.

More than she should.

"Yes. It is. Thank you for checking on me and for making sure I understood that everybody is allowed to make mis-takes. I felt pretty bad."

"All right. I suppose that this might be a good time to tell you that you have egg in your hair, and there's been a piece of bacon on your shoulder all morning." He grinned. "Peter and I have had a little bet going, as to whether or not that was going to last until ten o'clock, when the rush ended. I wouldn't bet farther than that, because I knew you'd have time after that to go change."

"You're kidding!" she exclaimed, stepping back and feeling a little bad that his arms dropped, not knowing whether to be upset or to laugh, because she did indeed have egg and bacon on her. "I'm going to do one better than change my clothes. I'm going to take a shower. You guys can hold down the fort until I get back."

"Be sure to clock out," Elias said as she started to walk away.

"I think I'm going to make the owner pay for this. After all, she's the one who forced a man who feels like a brick wall when you run into him to work here. If it hadn't been for that, I would have walked right through you, and then the breakfasts would have been saved."

"I think she just complimented me," Elias said, looking at Peter who had an eyebrow raised.

"She definitely complimented you. Brick wall? I'll take that." The little man stuck his chest out, but unfortunately, he did not quite look like a brick wall.

"You might want to keep working on that," Elias said with a grin.

"I'm thinking it may be hopeless, but my wife likes me the way I am, so I'm not too worried about it."

"All right. I'll let you guys continue to talk about...whatever it is that you're talking about, and I'll be back."

She walked out of the room, still smiling. Yes, life had definitely gotten a lot more interesting since Elias started working at the diner.

Chapter 19

Elias finished wiping the last table and put the rag in the pan, carrying the heavy load of dirty dishes back to the kitchen.

"This is the last one," he said as he walked in.

Peter had gone home thirty minutes ago, and Elias had actually been supposed to go home even earlier. But he wasn't going to let Jane stay and finish up by herself.

He couldn't believe that she worked from the time the diner opened until it closed at night, all day every day.

She usually took a few hours in the middle of the afternoon when things were slow, after her daughters got home from school, to check on them, look at their homework, and talk about their day.

Then the girls came down to the diner and ate supper down there.

Jane often stopped what she was doing and ate with them, if things weren't too busy.

Otherwise, she was on her feet, constantly working.

"That's fantastic. I am definitely ready to be done today," she said, putting the last pot away and wiping the stove.

He dragged his feet because he'd gotten used to walking her out.

Maybe it was his imagination, but she seemed to like it when he did.

Typically they got done together, and he had to admit that was partly his timing. He did it on purpose.

"You know you don't have to wait." She didn't look around at him as she put the garbage bag back in the garbage can.

"I know."

An animal sound shattered the silence that had descended.

"What was that?" he said automatically, thinking it sounded like an elephant that had a cold.

The sound came again.

"I'm pretty sure that's Billy. Sounds like he's right out front." Jane raised her brows at him and gave him a look that said she had no idea what was going on.

"Should we check on him? He sounds sick. Or like he's in some kind of distress."

She huffed a little laugh. "That's the way cows sound when they bawl, but it is kind of weird that he's doing it and it sounds like it's right outside my door."

"That is strange." He thought it was probably silly of him to ask if Billy would break the window trying to get in. It would just show that he knew nothing about animals. She didn't seem to be worried about it, and surely it wasn't going to be a problem, or she would have said something.

"I'm going to grab an apple, just in case," Jane said as he turned to walk out.

"An apple?" He couldn't help it. He stopped and turned around to look at her, thinking she might be a little crazy. "What are you going to do? Throw it at him?"

"No. Sometimes cows like apples. Not all cows. I think it just depends on how adventurous they are if they've never had one."

"I wouldn't have given any cow the label of adventurous, but if you say so."

"I do." She grinned at him, and he couldn't help himself, and he grinned back.

It was funny the way she made him laugh. The way she made him feel like life wasn't nearly as serious as what he'd felt it was for so long.

He could see now, when he was in the military, how seriously he had taken everything.

Of course he had. He had planned to make a career out of it, and he didn't want to take a single misstep.

But coming to Sweet Water, and to Jane's diner in particular, had shown him a gentler, more casual way to live. He had to admit he liked Jane's way.

As much as she worked, as much as she was on her feet from the time she got up until she went to bed at night, as much as she seemed to drive herself, she still laughed, had fun, and teased smiles from other people.

He'd seen her do it with the diner patrons, and she'd done it to him. Her easy-going, calm way of handling things.

She held herself to a high standard, true. And he saw that when she had run into him and dropped all the food.

But her grace toward others was unparalleled along with her kindness in the face of people being rude.

There had been several diners he had wanted to grab a hold of, and Jane just kept smiling, kept doing everything in her power to make them happy and give them a good experience.

He would have thought that that would give people license to take advantage of her, but on the contrary, the townspeople seemed to rally around her, love her, and defend her.

He hadn't ever articulated it, but he'd almost seen kindness as a weakness. Particularly kindness in the face of un-kindness. If someone was unkind to him, his tendency was to want to write them off, but Jane didn't do that. She lived what the Bible said.

He stopped with his hand on the door-knob, squinting out into the dark night.

"There's a light switch right here," Jane said as she flipped it and the outside lights came on, showing a shaggy head and equally shaggy body standing on the sidewalk looking right in the diner door.

"It was dark in here. What made him think that he could look in here and get anything?"

"I don't know. It'd be different if I fed him a lot, but I never do. I don't think I've ever fed him from this side."

"I've seen you take stuff, and Sorrell said you were feeding Billy."

"Yeah." She smiled. "We name our cows around here. It's a town cow because it has a name."

He laughed, assuming that the cows out on the range probably didn't have names. There were too many of them to keep track of, he assumed.

"Most of the things I set out are for the pig, since cows don't eat the things that I typically have. Once in a while, we have sweet corn in the summer, and I'm sure he'll eat that. But the pig will too, so they might have a fight over it."

"The rumors I heard was that the cow was in love with the pig."

"Billy does chase Munchy around an awful lot. And he does seem to have a huge attachment to her. Munchy, on the other hand, doesn't seem to like Billy much at all."

"Munchy is the name of the pig?" he asked, just to be sure.

"Yep."

That had no sooner come out of her mouth than the cow bawled again.

He managed not to jump. "Wow. That's loud. It's not like a little moo that I thought cows made."

"No. Sometimes mama cows will make a lowing sound. I think that's probably where the moo that we always think of comes from."

"You seem to be an expert on cows."

"No. Far from it. I just know a little bit from hanging out with friends who have farms. Nothing from my own experience."

"I see. Well, I don't even have friends who have farms." He paused. "Except, now I do. But we haven't had it long enough for me to learn anything like that. Plus, we don't have cows at all."

"No, but I suppose you could tell me about airplanes." She looked at him from under her brows, and he jerked his head in acknowledgment.

But he didn't say anything. His experience in the Air Force had left a sour taste in his mouth, and though he had joined thinking that he might fly planes, he supposed he left with the idea that he hadn't been given a fair shake. Maybe that was why he hadn't been very interested in the business his friends were doing. Crop dusting would require flying.

"Come on. We'll see if he'll take an apple and see if we can tell if there's anything wrong."

As soon as he opened the door, he realized he should have grabbed his coat. It was cold out.

"Do you think he's cold?" he asked as Jane walked out and he closed the door behind her.

"Look at that coat. He couldn't possibly be cold. I wish I had a coat like that."

He looked at Billy's coat, shaggy and long, although it did look pretty comfortable. It also looked so thick and warm that he couldn't possibly be cold. Even though the wind was blowing.

"Hey, Billy. Are you hungry? Why are you standing here bawling?" Jane said, talking to him like he was a person.

That was interesting. He'd heard that people talked to their pets, but he figured it was dogs and cats. Why would someone talk to a cow?

"So is there a reason you're talking to him? Please tell me that you don't actually expect him to understand you, correct?"

He probably was so deeply besotted with her that he really didn't care if she talked to cows or not.

Not that his infatuation was going to go anywhere. He always needed to remind himself of that.

"Of course he doesn't understand. He's a cow." Jane looked at him like he was crazy. "Just, sometimes when you talk, it calms animals down. The tone of your voice. It doesn't really matter what you say. I could have come out here and started reciting algebra facts and said them in a sweet, kind tone, and it would have been just as good. For him. For me, I like to make sense when I talk. And I don't recite algebra facts unless I'm at gunpoint."

He huffed a laugh. "I'll remember that."

"Yeah. I might have to rope you into helping my daughters with their homework, just like I roped you into starting to work for me, if you're still around when they take algebra."

"What makes you think I'm any better at it than you are?"

She grinned at him, and he liked that look. "I have a hunch."

"I'm sworn to secrecy."

"Well, in that case, I've heard that it will never get out."

He couldn't believe she was joking about him being dishonorably discharged and everything that had gone on with that.

And even more amazing was the fact that he was laughing with her.

He heard himself and didn't feel the slightest bit upset about it, but there was a part of his brain that just couldn't believe he was laughing.

"Billy, want an apple?" Jane asked, walking closer to the cow and holding her hand out.

Billy held his big head up and sniffed the apple, then took it gently from her hand.

"I thought for a moment your hand was going to disappear in his mouth."

"I'm safe. Cows don't have front teeth on the upper part of their jaw. So they're not going to bite you. I mean, if you put your hand in their mouth, and they get you with their back teeth, I imagine it would hurt. But I've never heard of that happening."

"I see. So it takes some effort to get bitten by a cow."

"I would say so." She lifted her shoulder, but she pulled in a bit, looking like she was cold.

He was sure she was.

"Their tongues are pretty strong. And they're also very grippy. They can really grab a hold of something, and if they get a hold of you with their tongue and you're not paying attention, they can grab your hand and pull it into their mouth. That's happened to me once. Since then, I've been more careful."

"With a small child, they could probably get an arm."

"Yeah. They wouldn't find a small child's arm tasty, though, so I don't think you have to worry about any of your children being eaten by a cow."

"There are no children," he said, knowing that she probably knew that but just clearing the air in case she didn't.

"Well. Now you know for the future." She grinned and then stepped closer to Billy, putting her hands in his fur coat. "You're warm, Billy. It's cold outside tonight."

"Yeah. We should have brought coats."

"I didn't even think. And I should have. I've been in North Dakota long enough to know it's dumb to walk outside after September without assuming that you're going to need a jacket."

"That early?"

"We can have some really nice days in September, but around here, it's better to be safe than sorry. Just take a jacket." She grinned. "We can go inside in a minute, or you can go on in. I just wanted to check him out a little bit and make sure there wasn't anything seriously wrong. I don't see any blood." She put her hands on the steer, petting him but also looking around, looking at his legs, feeling down his stomach.

Elias watched her. There was something fascinating about her hands, about the way she moved, about how gentle she was and careful. How she cared.

She touched all the places in his heart, places he hadn't even realized could be touched.

And he found himself fascinated by her.

But watching her as she moved around, he realized she was shivering for real, and he wanted her to get finished so he could get her inside.

They'd already turned the heat down in the downstairs part of the diner. They did that about fifteen minutes before the last patron left.

Jane had grinned and said that she liked to save money wherever she could. And he couldn't fault her for that.

As soon as the dining area cleared out, it cooled down, and there was no point in keeping it heated to a temperature that would make people who were sitting down comfortable.

And for him, he was walking around so much that he never got cold. In fact, he typically worked in a T-shirt so he didn't sweat all over everyone.

Regardless, she would need to go upstairs in order to get warm.

She didn't seem bothered though and didn't complain about the cold. Her teeth just chattered, and she finally stilled, stopping at the steer's front shoulder and scratching his neck.

"I don't see anything wrong. It's just so odd that he's out here bawling."

He couldn't stand it any longer, she was freezing, and while he was cold, he wasn't shivering.

He stepped over. Standing behind her, putting his arms around her. He touched the steer with his hands and didn't hold her, but he said, "You look so cold."

He hadn't asked, but she didn't move away, didn't tell him that she minded.

"You're like a furnace back there."

"Good to know. I'm feeling chilly."

"I'm sorry. I just... It'd be terrible if anything happened to Billy, and I knew that there was a potential problem and hadn't checked it out."

"I'm not asking you to hurry. I'm just taking care of a problem that I saw."

"What was that?" she asked, sounding truly baffled.

"You were cold," he said softly.

"Oh." She seemed surprised. "Thank you."

Maybe he should be honest. He wasn't sure if he could say what he wanted to, without it coming out wrong, but he figured he might as well try.

"It's...not a hardship to stand here."

"Outside?"

"This close to you. I...wanted to be closer."

He was so inept. He couldn't get the right words to come out. Words to tell her that he wanted to stand there. That he wanted to put his arms around her. That her being cold was just an excuse.

Billy moved his head, shifting his front shoulder and pushing Jane.

"Oof!" she exclaimed, stumbling back into his chest.

His arms tightened around her, and he turned her the rest of the way around so she was facing him, pressed against his chest.

"Are you okay?" he asked, half wanting to thank the steer for pushing Jane. If he didn't know better, he would almost say the steer did it on purpose. Because now he stood there, calmly chewing his cud, like he hadn't moved at all.

And he had Jane in his arms. It wasn't exactly his goal when he woke up this morning, but it could have been.

"I'm sorry. That's the second time I've run into you today." Her words were said on a small laugh that was half grunt.

"I think I'm getting used to it. I caught you this time."

"I'll be really impressed when you catch me and the food I'm carrying."

"I guess if you want to practice, I could stay for another hour. Do I get paid for it?" he teased.

"Of course. I could never ask you to work for free even if you are just practicing," she said.

"I was kidding. You haven't had to pay me to stay extra, in case you haven't noticed."

"I have. Thank you."

Her arms came up and wrapped around his waist while his were wrapped around her, holding her close, giving her his heat, and although he could still feel her shivering, she wasn't shaking quite as violently as she had been.

"I'm not sure what to do about it."

"I guess I don't even really want to think about it. I don't dislike standing here. This is...the best part of the day so far."

She laughed. "I guess we should thank Billy, because I'm kind of enjoying it as well."

He didn't say anything more. They'd both admitted to enjoying it, liking it, but he thought they both knew that it couldn't be anything more.

He warred with himself. Did he want to make their friendship awkward? Because while he wasn't in any position to get married, and Jane really wasn't either, he wanted to be more than friends with her.

But it didn't seem fair to ask someone to be more than friends but less than someone he would consider marrying. And until he was ready to be married, it seemed wrong to walk into a relationship, knowing that he was going to have to ask whoever it was to wait on him.

For a long time. Possibly years.

"You've tensed. What are you thinking about?" Jane asked from where she was tucked in under his chin against his chest.

He liked feeling her breathe, liked the feel of her against him. And he didn't mean for them to, but his arms tightened.

"I don't know if I would make much sense, and I might be overstepping and a little out of line."

"Overstepping and out of line?" she asked, sounding baffled.

"I like standing here holding you. But I would like to take our relationship a little bit further, in the physical sense anyway. Kissing you. How's that for making something simple complicated?"

She didn't laugh like he thought she would, and she had tensed under his hands.

"It's fine. If you're not interested in kissing me, I had pretty much talked myself out of it."

"Why?"

He couldn't tell what she was thinking by the tone of her voice. "Because. I'm not in any position to get married. And I'm guessing you aren't either."

"I guess I didn't think you were asking me to marry you."

"I know. But when you take a relationship into the kissing stage, there ought to be some kind of endgame in sight, shouldn't there?"

"That's not necessarily something that a lot of people think anymore."

"I know. It's old-fashioned. I suppose it just seems a little disrespectful to expect someone to stay in a relationship indefinitely with you, with no intention of moving forward, a physical relationship with no point."

"Other than you like each other?"

"Well, there's that, but..." He could not explain what he meant.

"I understand. I guess I was giving you a little bit of a hard time, but I didn't need to. You're right. And I actually really admire that. It's wrong if you don't have intentions, good intentions, the right intentions, and you're entering into a relationship, assuming the person you're with is okay with going past the lines of friendship with no intention of marriage."

"That's right. I guess if I want to get into that kind of relationship, I would want to know that marriage was in my near future. I...don't want to be running around kissing girls that I don't have intentions toward. It seems...wrong."

"I agree with you. It is totally wrong. Because if you have no intention of marrying them, you know for a fact that you are kissing someone who's going to be someone else's husband or wife. And knowing that you're doing that just doesn't seem right."

"I've never heard it explained quite like that, but that would be my thought exactly. If you don't have intentions of moving forward, then you shouldn't be kissing."

They stood in silence for a bit, and even with them pressed together sharing heat, he knew she was still cold. He wondered why she didn't pull away.

Both of them said they weren't planning on getting married, and both of them agreed that a relationship without those kinds of plans was pointless.

And yet, here they both stood, wrapped in each other's arms.

"Why aren't you pulling away?" he asked finally.

"If I say it's because Billy is pressed up against my back, would you believe me?"

He laughed. "Really? You have a cow behind you and a rock wall in front of you, and you're stuck here, so you just have your hands wrapped around me for the kicks and giggles?"

"Mostly," she said, and he could hear the teasing in her tone.

He liked that, liked that they were still comfortable with each other and had been able to talk about something that maybe a lot of people might have skirted around.

It made him feel good that Jane was the kind of person not to skirt around the hard things.

Not that he was going to be doing any-thing with her anytime soon.

"I guess I never thanked you for hiring me," he finally said.

"That feels like it came out of the blue."

"Well, it's something I've been thinking about for a while. You know, since I started. You seem to bring out a lighter side of me. I...was in a terrible place, and I'd gotten...bitter. Was upset about the way things went down, that they were unfair. I was holding God accountable. And I've been thinking since I came here that sometimes He has to take something away, in order to give you something better."

She nodded. "Isn't it funny? We sit there like a little baby, throwing a fit over having a toy taken away, when God had to take the toy away in order to give us something even better."

"Yeah. I guess I was being a two-year-old, angry at God and wanting Him to give me back what I thought I deserved. To give the person who wouldn't come forward with the truth what they deserved."

"Through all that, you held onto your integrity."

"It was cold comfort when I saw my career crumble and had that emptiness of the rest of my life stretching out before me when I left the military."

"And now?"

"Yeah. And now, I feel like God wanted me to come to North Dakota, that a career in the Air Force wasn't what He wanted for me. Maybe what they say about time and distance lending perspective is true. Because I feel like that's what's happened to me, along with a good influence."

"Good influence?"

"You. You working hard but laughing while you do it."

"Wouldn't we all be miserable if I were miserable? If I go around miserable every day, you wouldn't want to come here and work. Or you'd hate it if you had to."

"You make people smile. That's admirable."

"You're saying it like it's something special. It's just something everybody does."

"Not on a daily basis. Most people put on a good front to impress people for a little bit, and then you find out what their true selves are. That's not the way you are. What you put on, what you show, that is really you."

She sighed. "I guess I had the same choice after my divorce. To get bitter about it, and hate him, and be upset that he didn't pay child support, and that he found someone else and all that. It hurt for a long time, but I didn't want to be angry. I wanted to be a happy person. I couldn't let him steal my joy. I just couldn't."

"I'm glad you made that decision. And, you know, you making the decision to not allow him to steal your joy, but to be happy in spite of him, affects everyone around you. Maybe it was a decision you made for yourself, but it became a decision that affects all the people who are in contact with you. Me, even though I didn't know you then."

"That's a good point. We don't realize how our decisions affect the people around us every day. Our decisions to do right. Our decisions to do hard things." She paused. "Your decision to keep your integrity and keep your word. Bet you anything that the person who asked you to keep that quiet has been affected by your actions."

He grunted. "Maybe."

"I guarantee it. They have to look at you and wonder what makes you so willing to take the pain and suffering rather than go back on your word."

"They probably think I'm every kind of a fool."

"Then that makes them the fool, doesn't it?"

She had a point. He couldn't deny it.

"Maybe I'm the fool for thinking that all I should be doing here is standing here holding you, because every time you talk to me like that, it feels like I should never let you go."

Chapter 20

Saturday, Jane sat at the community center, watching her girls play basketball with the other kids.

There wasn't anything serious about the game, but they'd all agreed to meet and Jane sat with her friend Ainsley, watching.

Ainsley didn't have any kids, but she heard Jane was going to watch her kids and said she'd like to come and just hang out, since they seldom got to do that outside of the diner.

Ainsley had a farmers market on Tuesdays when Jane closed the diner, and

Jane always worked Saturday nights because it was the most busy when Ainsley had off.

"I've heard rumors about your new hire, and they must be true, if you're taking a Saturday night off," Ainsley said as she removed her coat and hooked it over the back of her chair before she sat down.

"That's the truth. I... I didn't think I would ever trust anyone in the diner while I wasn't there, but I have to admit, he's...different."

"Different," Ainsley said, wiggling her brows.

"Oh, stop." She shook her head, smiling. "Nothing like that. He's too serious and isn't interested in marriage, any more than I am. You know I'm too busy. I can barely find time to spend with my girls."

Today had been a real blessing. She always tried to sneak more time with them, but it just seemed that the diner ate into everything. She finally closed it on Tuesdays, just so that she would have an entire evening to spend with them.

Now here she was taking Tuesday, Wednesday morning, and Saturday evening off.

"I'm starting to think you're slacking, with all this time you're taking off."

Jane laughed. "I don't. It feels weird to not be working, especially when there is work, I'm just not doing it."

"Are you nervous? You want to go check on it?" Ainsley grinned. "You know, like a mother leaving her kid at the sitters for the first time."

That made Jane laugh again. "That's a little bit what it feels like. But different, because I trust Elias. He's...different."

"I think you might have mentioned that already. Can you define 'different?'"

"I don't know. He's commanding. Just confident in himself, and he doesn't lord things over people, but he has a natural leadership type way about him. It's a natural draw that people just want to follow him, and they want to do what he tells them to. I can't understand it, and it's hard to explain, but it's true."

"He's just a waiter, right?" Ainsley asked. "I mean, you didn't sell the diner to him and not tell me?"

"Oh my goodness, no. Yes. He's just a waiter. Although not really. Because he does everything. He jumps in wherever there is a need, and doesn't wait for someone to tell him, and doesn't wait to get permission. And if he doesn't know how to do it, he figures it out."

"Well, good for him. I've heard that the other men out on the Sweet Briar Ranch are ex-Air Force too. Maybe that has something to do with it. Being in the Air Force?"

Jane nodded, not wanting to get into too many details. She didn't know what Elias was saying around town. But she knew he hadn't been eager to divulge the details of his past, and she didn't know what he didn't want spread, so she thought it would be best for her to just be quiet and let him say what he wanted.

That included the fact that he had been an officer, because she didn't want to have to say that he had been dishonorably discharged. He didn't sound like he was going to keep that a secret, but she didn't know. It probably wasn't the information that he wanted to lead with when he was developing relationships with people, at any rate.

"So how are things going with you?" she asked, knowing that anything that they talked about that had to do with Elias was shaky ground. Especially with Ainsley, since Ainsley knew her so well.

She clapped as Sorrell ran up, making a layup.

Ainsley looked down, and Jane touched her hand that was lying on the table between them. "What is it?"

"I don't know. I guess ever since Teagan and then Brooklyn got married, it's been...hard. I don't mean that in an oh, woe is me kind of way, but just a...a strange feeling."

"Like you're missing out?"

"That's it." She nodded, her expression saying she hadn't realized until just then. "That's it exactly. I was so happy when it was just the four of us. You know, we were working hard to make the ranch profitable, and now it's all different. It was like all of us together, and then we slowly started peeling off, and I don't know. I guess if I were one of the ones who left, I would look back on it with fondness, and I'd be looking forward to my new life. But being that I'm one of the ones who were..."

"Left behind?"

"Yeah. I hate to say it like that, but that's exactly right. One of the ones that were left behind. And it just feels sad. Even though Teagan comes back lots to visit, and Brooklyn is still really involved in the business. It's just...quiet in the house at night."

"I can only imagine. Probably a little lonely as well."

"Yeah. Zaylee and I have been talking about it, and we're both thinking that maybe we should just sell the farm. Maybe Brooklyn and Cormac would want to buy it. Or, I don't know, maybe Teagan and Deuce would when they come back. I just hate to see it go to someone else, but it's really hard to keep trucking on when things have changed so much."

Jane's heart went out to her friend. That would be so hard. She had all those changes, in such a short amount of time, especially when she and her sisters were bonded as closely as they were.

"I bet when your sisters start having children, and they start coming around, you'll be like a big, happy family again.

And maybe, you'll get to the point where you enjoy the quiet evenings where there's not quite so much activity. A time of rest and quietness."

She knew she was grasping at straws, trying to give Ainsley something to look forward to. That was so important in a person's life. Having something to look forward to.

She clapped again as Merritt stole the ball. She didn't make a basket with it, but she did have an awesome pass to a teammate who made a hoop, which showed that her confidence was growing.

"I know. But I'll probably feel the same if they're having children and I'm not. I just... I guess that I thought we'd be together forever. And seeing them happy with husbands has kind of made me long for one too. But there's just no time, especially with them gone. More work falls on our shoulders, and...I don't know. Sometimes I think having a new start might be the best thing."

"I suppose if that's what you feel. But it makes me sad to hear you say that, because you know I'd miss you if you decide to leave and go anywhere. You know I'll support you whatever you do though. And sometimes new things are scary and sad, but they turn out to be the very best things. You know?"

"That's what I was thinking. I want to look at it more as a new beginning than anything else. But I guess I'm still waiting on God's timing. He just doesn't seem to be opening any doors, and every time I think about leaving, I feel like I hear Him whispering, 'just stay.'"

"Then that's what you better do," Jane said. "I know what you mean. I was divorced for a while before I felt God saying it was okay for me to move. And it just so happened that this diner was up for sale, and the amount that I had saved was enough to purchase it. If I had run ahead, trying to do something different, I know it wouldn't have worked out. God can take our mistakes and turn them for our good and His glory, but I would rather just do it His way to begin with. It saves a lot of pain and makes things easier."

"I agree. And thank you. When we're waiting on God it sometimes feels like a long time. But it's nice to hear that you waited. And it worked out. Sometimes I think I'll just be waiting here forever, waiting until I'm old, and still waiting. But maybe, that's just what I need to do. Until God shows me something different."

"I think that's probably the most important reason to be in your Bible and praying, because a lot of times, God shows us through His Word what He wants from us. We just have to have the discernment to see it. And praying that God will open our eyes to what we're reading and let us know what His will is."

"Yeah, that's a good reminder. I guess I've been focusing on my discontent and what I can do to fix it, and less on what God's going to do. And maybe, what He wants to do with my discontent is just for me to turn it into contentment."

"That might be true," Jane said, and she thought about herself. She'd been fine, had been perfectly content focusing on raising her girls and making the diner a success until Elias showed up.

Since then, she found herself day-dreaming about him, thinking about taking time off from the diner, and family things. Not that she hadn't wanted to be a family with the girls before, but she had been content to work and give them the evenings. But now... She didn't know. She just felt alive in a way she couldn't explain. Like things might be going to change soon, and she was ready for it.

Ainsley mentioned not seeing Munchy, the pig that roamed the streets of Sweet Water, around for a while, and the conversation took a different turn, with Jane tucking her thoughts back in the back of her mind.

She needed to enjoy her friendship with Elias and not think about anything else. Just focus on raising her girls, since that was the reason she bought the diner in the first place, and make the diner her second priority, but still give it the importance that it needed, making sure that it was as successful as she could make it.

Chapter 21

Jane couldn't keep the silly grin off her face, and she hummed as she worked in the kitchen, making popcorn and pulling some cookies out of a bag from the freezer and warming them up in the microwave.

Soon, her kitchen smelled amazing, popcorn and cookies.

Pouring three glasses of milk, she decided to carry them in with a flourish, so she used a plate since she didn't have any fancy trays and arranged the cookies in a cute pattern on the plate.

Reminding herself that she was going to say yes more often than she said no to her girls, she walked into the room.

They settled down, the popcorn between them, lying on blankets, with their pillows propped behind them, munching and chatting.

Jane realized that her girls were growing up, and they were turning into people that she actually liked. She enjoyed spending time with them and vowed again to make sure that she said yes to more requests.

Chatting about the different recipes that they had tried at the diner, not talking about the diner in a work-related way but in a way where the girls wanted to spend more time with her, experimenting in the kitchen and helping her cook.

She hadn't realized that was something that they wanted, and she was all for it.

She visualized the day when the three of them worked in the diner together. Maybe with their husbands as her girls grew up and got married.

Not that she didn't want a better future for them, if there was something else that they wanted to do, but she didn't place a high premium on jobs that required a lot of education, the way the rest of the world did.

She wouldn't discourage them from doing that, if that's what they wanted, but she didn't feel that those kinds of jobs were any better than jobs that didn't take education. It depended on what a person wanted out of their life and, more importantly, what God wanted them to do.

"Merritt and I want to cook for you the Tuesday after next. When you're off and we don't have anything scheduled. We want to make supper," Sorrell said, and she kind of stumbled a little.

That made Jane's heart break just a little. The fact that Sorrell was unsure about asking her if she could cook and saying that she wanted to make supper.

"You work hard, Mom, and we wanted you to have a night off. We think we can make something that will be good, and we just wanted you to be able to relax and enjoy it, instead of having to work on your day off."

Merritt sounded so sweet. Such a thoughtful thing. Jane smiled, even though she wanted to say no, because a lot of times when the kids were in the kitchen, it ended up being more work for her to clean up than it was for her to just do it herself.

She said, "That's so sweet of you guys. Of course you can do that."

"So you need to do something that Tuesday afternoon, like...go to the spa or something."

"There's no spa in Sweet Water." Jane's brows furrowed. That was weird. What did her girls know about a spa anyway?

"You could go to Rockerton. Get your hair done. You know, maybe your nails too," Sorrell said eagerly.

"They'll even do your makeup. At least that's what Toni said."

"What made you girls think about wearing makeup?" Jane asked, confused. Why would her girls be talking about make-up?

Was she that far behind the times? Did ten-year-olds think about makeup now?

"We didn't say for us, Mom. We said for you!" Sorrell said, like Jane was totally not getting it.

She supposed she wasn't since she had misunderstood. She knew they were talking about her, but it just seemed odd. She wasn't really the type of woman who ever went to a spa. In fact, she couldn't remember the last time she got her hair done and her nails and her makeup and went out.

It had been...a decade or more.

"I don't know, guys. That sounds kind of...a lot. It's one thing for you to cook for me, that's fine and I'm looking forward to it, but I guess I would rather spend the afternoon reading a book somewhere than going and getting all of that stuff done."

Her girls look distressed.

Even in the flickering candlelight, she could see that.

"Did you guys want to go with me?" she asked, hardly daring to believe it and careful not to sound like she was willing to take them.

They were just nine and ten.

But they were growing up faster than she wanted them to, and she supposed children started younger than they used to. But they still played with baby dolls. It was so weird to think about her girls wanting to experiment with makeup.

"No. We're going to be cooking supper."

"All afternoon?"

"Not all afternoon, but it's going to take us a couple hours, and we're going to clean the house too," Merritt volunteered, but Sorrell seemed like she wanted to shush her, and Jane smiled.

They were trying to keep this a secret, bless their little hearts.

"All right. I'll be out of the apartment. I'm not promising to go get my hair or nails or anything done, but I'll take a good book with me and maybe go to the church and sit in the back of the pew and just read for a bit or something, okay?"

Maybe she could pray. She hadn't had uninterrupted time to pray by herself for a really long time. At night when she tried to do it, she fell asleep. In the morning, it seemed like her feet hit the floor and immediately there were a hundred things that needed her attention.

It would be nice to just sit in the back pew of the church, enjoy the silence, and talk to God. She was long overdue for a chat with Him.

"I still think you should treat yourself. Get your hair done and all that other stuff that women do once in a while to make themselves look pretty and attractive."

She had no desire to do that, but her girls seemed set on it. And maybe it was because they were going to clean the apartment and make a fancy meal and they wanted her to look the part.

She supposed she could do that. She didn't really want to. The idea of sitting in the back pew of the church and just being with God for a little bit was much more appealing to her, but she just said that she wasn't going to tell her girls no, and she wanted to keep her word and do what she said. Plus, it seemed to mean a lot to them.

"All right. I'll at least go get my hair cut. How's that?"

"Get them to do your makeup while you're there."

"Do salons do that?" Maybe that's why they call it a beauty salon.

"Toni said they did."

"What does Toni know about all of this stuff?"

"She likes makeup," Sorrell said, shrugging.

"Does her mom know that?"

"I think so. She said she was allowed to wear it around the house, but she wasn't allowed to wear it when they went anywhere until she was fourteen."

"I see."

She supposed her girls would be fourteen before she realized it, and maybe Mallie was right to let them experiment.

Of course, her girls hadn't asked to experiment. They wanted her to go so they could make a nice meal for her and clean the house. How sweet.

"All right. It's a deal. Are you guys sure you'll be okay here by yourselves?"

She had left them by themselves more than once, but usually it was just when she was downstairs at the diner, and they were upstairs in the apartment.

Which wasn't really like leaving them by themselves, it was like having them upstairs when she was downstairs.

Still, she'd gone to get groceries and other things while they'd stayed home. So she knew they would be fine, but still, Rockerton was a ways away.

"Mom. We'll be fine. And if anything happens with the stove, Miss Mallie said that she would be on speed dial for us."

"So I assume Toni is helping with this?"

"Of course. She does everything with us."

"She's not here now," Jane felt compelled to point out.

"That's because it's family time, Mom," Sorrell said, sounding a little superior, but then her tone dropped. "It would be nice to have a dad when we do family time."

They hadn't thrown the dad thing at her for a while. Jane had kinda thought they forgot about it. They used to ask about it a good bit, but they'd quit.

"If God wants me to have a husband and for you guys to have a dad, I hope He'll help us find the perfect man. In the meantime, we're going to be happy with what He's given us, because it's so very much, we have so much to be thankful for."

The girls nodded, and she knew that they agreed with her. They'd talked over and over again about how blessed they were to have a roof over their heads, one that didn't leak, and a business and honest labor, and a community that rallied around people.

And she had girls who wanted to make her happy. Even if it wasn't exactly what she wanted to do, she would do it for them, to make them feel good.

Chapter 22

"I'm a greeter today, and I won't be able to sit with you." Gideon slapped Elias's shoulder as they walked toward the church.

The wind blew dried grass and other debris across the sidewalk as they walked, but from what Elias had been told, they were lucky it wasn't snowing. As cold as the wind felt, snow would make it even colder.

"I'm actually the monitor for junior church, so I won't be in the service either," Jonah said from behind them.

"That's all right. My first day in church, and I'm winging it on my own. No problem." Elias really didn't mind being by himself.

He wasn't exactly a loner, but being alone never bothered him. A lot of times, he had to be alone in order to forge the way forward.

Although teamwork and brotherhood were everything in the military, sometimes leaders had a lonely job.

Of course, that was his old life.

They hadn't come to church in the last two weeks he'd been there, so this was his first Sunday at Sweet Water's church.

He couldn't help but wonder if Jane would be there.

They hadn't talked about church while he'd been working at the diner, although he would definitely say she was a Christian and a spiritual one at that.

She was very conscientious, trying to do right.

He supposed he was judging by her life and not by her saying it, which was probably a better indicator of a true Christian than anything, when a person had a life that pointed to Jesus, not words that gave lip service to a religion a person didn't really follow.

That had been him for a long time. He called himself a Christian, but he didn't always act like it. Usually didn't act like it.

It was a relief when they walked into the vestibule out of the wind and cold.

Gideon disappeared without saying anything, although Jonah smacked his arm and said, "You good?"

Elias jerked his head.

All he needed to do was find an empty seat and sit down.

"Elias!" a woman's voice said.

Elias thought he saw a smirk on Jonah's face before he turned and walked away, but he couldn't be sure.

He turned to look at Miss April. "Miss April. It's good to see you here."

He meant that too. It was nice to see a familiar face. It was a little disconcerting, even for someone with confidence like his, to walk into a building full of strangers.

Of course, as he looked around, he recognized a lot of the faces from people that he'd served at the diner.

Some of them even smiled and waved at him. With a few of them, he even knew their names.

"It's so good to see you here. This is your first Sunday, isn't it?"

"Yes, ma'am," he said.

"Well then, you need someone to show you around," she said, grabbing his arm and pulling him forward.

He went, bemused. He could have found his way around on his own, but he supposed if they had someone assigned to do this type of duty, he was fine with it.

His eyes swept the sanctuary again, looking one more time to see if he could find Jane.

That's who he really wanted to see.

"Piper!" Miss April said, drawing his attention back to the people immediately in front of him.

Piper, the single mom he'd met with Miss April more than a week ago, stood, looking frazzled as she held a crying baby in one hand, a diaper bag in the other along with what he assumed was her Bible, while her toddler grabbed at her legs, and the same little boy who'd opened the door when they visited ran in circles around her, singing something.

Her other three children were not in sight. At least, not that Elias could tell.

Of course, if he were old enough to take care of himself, he would probably want to walk away from that noise and chaos as well.

The kids would have to be a little bit older before they would think to help with it, rather than leave it.

"Piper, this is Elias's first day at church, and I was hoping that you would be able to show him around."

Piper looked confused.

"You mean help him find a seat?" she asked, over the crying baby.

"No. You know, give him a tour of the church. He needs to know where the restrooms are in case he needs to go to the little boys' room," Miss April said.

Elias felt his cheeks warming. Amazing. At his age.

Still, he hadn't heard it called the little boys' room in a really long time. And the fact that Miss April was obviously asking Piper to do something that was certainly going to put her out made him want to step in and say something.

But he didn't want to hurt Piper's feelings by making her feel like he didn't want to be led around the church by her. It wasn't that. He wasn't embarrassed at the crying kids, and he didn't hate her or anything. It was just... She obviously had more than enough to handle and didn't need anything extra.

But Miss April was already thanking her for helping out. "God blesses those who work in His house," she said as she patted Piper's shoulder and walked away.

"Sorry about the noise," Piper said, jiggling the baby in her arms and swooping down to try to pick up the toddler and juggle him and the baby bag and her Bible.

He felt like he should offer to carry something, but not a kid. That would only make them cry more. And the way she was holding everything, it would be a major undertaking for her to undo the baby bag from her shoulder and out from under the baby.

"You really don't have to show me around."

"I'm going downstairs anyway, and I can show you where the bathrooms are. It's about ten minutes until the service starts, so we have plenty of time." Piper's voice sounded tired, even with the baby's cries almost drowning it out.

"All right. After you."

She went down the stairs. He followed her and waited while she dropped her baby off at the nursery. There were several other babies and toddlers in there, but she picked up her own toddler and headed toward another room.

"This is the toddler Sunday school room," she said as she opened the door. "You can come in if you want, but you might want to wait outside."

He took one look at the chaos in there, figured he wasn't ready for that kind of initiation into church, and said, "I'll be here when you get back out."

She laughed a little and then disappeared.

It didn't take long before she was back out and dropped the little boy off in a different room.

"Now. The restrooms are back here," she said, going down a short hallway that was a little bit more deserted and slightly dark. "There's some unfinished rooms here and some rooms that they don't use unless they're having a special meeting or something. That's why everything's so dark. The only thing back here are the bathrooms."

"Okay. That explains why it's so dark and a lot quieter back here."

Piper stopped, pointing out the men's room and the ladies' room. And then she said, "I'm sorry about that. It seems like when you have six kids, one of them is always having a crisis. And usually it's pretty loud."

"That's okay. I wasn't complaining, I was just commenting."

"I don't even know why Miss April asked me. Except, it seems like it might be for the same reason she brought you to my house, and it's a little embarrassing for me, because I didn't ask for that."

"I didn't either. Just so we're clear." Elias offered her a tentative smile, and she returned it.

"All right. I worried about that a little bit, like you thought I might have gone to the ladies and tried to get them to coerce you to come to my house or something." She sighed, looking frazzled and overwhelmed, and Elias felt pity for her. "I just didn't want that on top of everything else." She took a deep breath. "I'm sorry. This is my husband's and my wedding anniversary. It's the second one I've spent without him, and it's no easier than the first. Just so many hopes and dreams gone. And just so much work and struggle stretching out in front of me as far as I can see."

And then, to Elias's horror, she started to cry.

"Hey. Don't do that." He knew those were stupid words to say. She didn't want to stand in the hallway in the church and cry over her dead husband any more than he wanted to stand here and watch her, but he didn't know what else to do. Reaching out, he put a hand on her shoulder, instinctively knowing that touch was a great comfort but not knowing how to give a touch that wasn't inappropriate. A hug would be nice, but it would feel awkward. For him anyway. He wasn't used to hugging people.

Except, holding Jane in his arms hadn't felt bad at all. He'd liked that. In fact, he wouldn't mind doing it again. But he didn't want to go around hugging any-one. For him, things like that were like what he had talked to Jane about. Kissing. It wasn't something he did with just anyone.

"I'm sorry." Piper sniffed, waving her hand in the air like she was trying to get herself to stop crying by motioning with her hands or something. He wasn't sure. "It's just been a really hard morning. And I don't know why I'm talking to you. I don't even know you."

"I'm just here. And you finally got rid of the kids. You probably couldn't break down in front of them." He was really guessing on that one.

"No. I could never do that."

Reluctantly, he put his other hand on her shoulder. Not wanting to leave her, but not having any idea how to deal with this. He tried to get her to look at him, because he wanted to let her know that he was going to leave and find someone who would be able to help her.

Just then, Jane came out of the ladies' restroom. She was alone, so he could only imagine that she walked down the stairs with her kids to the Sunday school rooms and then used the restroom herself.

Whatever happened, he found himself smiling, a goofy, silly grin that showed how much he felt for her. He knew he should try to wipe it off his face, but he didn't want to. He wanted her to know.

But the smile that had started to form on her face froze as her eyes traveled from him to Piper, then his hands on Piper's shoulders, then back to him.

In a flash, the idea that they were in a dark hallway, that they were alone, that it was private, and neither one of them looked like they were heading toward a bathroom or away from one, which would be the only reason two people should be in this abandoned dark hall-way, flew through his mind, and he realized what Jane was probably inferring by looking at their positions, and him touching her, and Piper with her head tucked down just an inch or so from his chest.

He hadn't been doing anything wrong.

At least he hadn't been intending to.

"Mr. Stone," Jane said, very formally. Like they barely knew each other and hadn't spent almost every day together since he moved to this town.

"Piper," she said, and her voice was slightly less chill. But she didn't look at them again as she squeezed behind Piper and walked back down the hall.

"Jane!" he said, taking his hands off Piper's shoulders and taking one step after her.

But he didn't want to leave Piper alone in the hall. Not in the shape that she was in.

He wasn't sure Jane was going to stop. She hadn't looked very happy with him. To be fair, if he had found her in the same position with a man, he wouldn't have been very happy with her either.

But she stopped. Maybe she responded to the urgency in his voice, or maybe she just responded because she felt the same thing for him that he felt for her. Something that went a little bit beyond just wanting to be friends. Or maybe a lot beyond. He hadn't figured it out yet.

"Yes?" she asked, turning slightly but staring at the wall and not looking at him.

"Would you mind staying here with Piper while I go find someone who can help her? Unless you can?"

"I'm fine," Piper said, sniffing.

Maybe it was the sniff, or maybe it was the crack in her voice that said plainly that she was crying, that made Jane turn, completely changing the expression on her face to one of total concern and compassion.

"Oh, Piper?" She hurried to Piper. "This was about the time that you and your husband were married, isn't it? Is it your anniversary?"

How did women remember those kinds of things? Not that he would have been expected to, having only met Piper once before in his life, but it amazed him how Jane seemed to intuitively know exactly what the problem was.

"Today," Piper said, holding herself in check until Jane wrapped her arms around her, and then she started sobbing. Big, wracking sobs that really made

Elias think that if he had been uncomfortable before, it was nothing compared to how he felt now. He wanted to run out of the church.

"Go ahead. You have every right in the world to cry. If you don't mind, I'm going to cry with you," Jane said, and as he looked at her face, he saw it was true. Her eyes filled with tears that spilled over down her cheeks.

She had empathy and compassion, and...he felt cold. Not unfeeling, just unable to allow himself to cry with someone he barely knew, or hold them, or empathize with them.

He supposed it was something that he needed to learn. Although he knew, almost instinctively, that if it had been

Jane crying in the hallway, he would have held her without a qualm, and while he might not have cried with her, it was quite possible that he might have.

"Do you want me to get someone else?" he asked softly, not wanting to interrupt whatever they were doing.

Jane shook her head no. "Maybe we'll sit in one of the Sunday school rooms for a bit and chat. If we need someone else, I'll either text you, or I'll go myself."

"Thanks," he said, and she nodded. She opened her mouth like she wanted to say something more, but she closed it and gave him a little smile.

He returned it and figured that everything was okay.

Going back upstairs, he found a seat in the sanctuary.

Chapter 23

He'd been out of church too long and really needed to hear the Word. He hadn't realized how much, until he had sat under the preaching and realized it was exactly what he needed. It was like the preacher had written the sermon just for him.

Of course, he'd always heard that when a person had a heart for the Lord, they would be sure to get something out of any sermon, even if it wasn't what the pastor had intended or what their neighbor got. It was what God spoke to them about.

Feeling like he'd had a spiritual workout by the time the sermon was over and he walked out of church, he wasn't paying much attention to the people around him, but thinking about what he had heard, when he heard his name.

"Elias!"

He recognized that voice, and he smiled. "Jane."

"Sorry about earlier in the hall."

"You don't have to apologize. I know how it looked. I... I should thank you for not running off in a huff but for taking a minute to listen and realize what was going on."

"I should have done it to begin with. I just... I guess I don't know what happened. But I'm sorry."

"Hey. No problem. Honest. Thanks for taking care of it. I... I was way out of my depth. And I was really thankful you stopped and came back to help me."

"Yeah. Thanks for asking me. You could have just let me go. I probably deserved it, since I was judging you without getting the whole story."

"We do that a lot, don't we?"

She nodded, and she seemed to understand that he meant we as in people, and everyone. Not just her and him. "We do. I guess it's a natural human thing. We have to train ourselves to think that maybe things aren't the way they appear or that maybe they're better."

"It's a hard thing. It's a human nature thing to assume the worst about people."

"It is for me."

He liked how she challenged him. Because she had admitted right away that she had been thinking the wrong thing and had apologized.

Apologizing wasn't easy and was something that he wasn't very good at. He supposed he could learn from her example and be humble. Because that's basically what apologizing was. Being humble.

Of course, there was a whole new level of humble, when someone apologized for something that they didn't feel was their fault, but they took the blame for it anyway.

That was the kind of humbleness of Christ on the cross.

He definitely hadn't gotten to that point yet.

"All right, what are you thinking?" Jane said, her lips tilting up in a grin.

"Just thinking about how much I appreciate that you're humble enough to apologize. It's really nice to be around someone who doesn't have to be right all the time, and not only that, but can step up to the plate when it's their fault and admit it."

"Jane," Cassie said, coming up beside her friend.

"Hey!" She smiled at her friend, then turned back to him. "I'll see you later."

He jerked his head. Maybe it was his imagination, or maybe it was just wishful thinking, but he thought he saw a little bit of disappointment on Jane's face as she watched him for a moment before she turned back to her friend and started chatting.

He walked away with a smile. There was just something about Jane that made him want to grin. He wasn't sure what it was, but the desire to be with her hadn't dissipated. In fact, if anything, it had gotten stronger.

He was in the parking lot when a child's voice stopped him.

"Mr. Elias?"

He turned around to see three little girls, Sorrell and Merritt and one other. The one who hung around them a lot and he recognized, but he didn't know her name.

"Yeah?" he asked, smiling at the girls. They were sweet, and he liked them. Of course, the fact that Sorrell and Merritt were Jane's girls probably made him like them a little bit more than normal.

Sorrell stepped forward. "We have something we want to ask you."

"All right. Go ahead."

He couldn't imagine what they wanted, but he knew he would have a hard time saying no to anything they asked.

"We wanted to have you over for dinner."

"The only night your mom has off is Tuesday night."

"I know. We can't do it this Tuesday, because we have basketball tryouts at school. But we were hoping we could do it next Tuesday. Would that be okay?" She seemed kind of eager and a little anxious. It was unlike the Sorrell he was used to in the diner where she was comfortable, laughed, and even joked with him.

"All right. At the diner?" he asked, just to be sure.

"No. In our apartment upstairs."

Did Jane get them to ask? His heart beat a little harder at the thought. "Does your mom know about this?"

"We want it to be a surprise. She knows we're cooking, but we didn't want you to say anything."

He wasn't sure what that was about, but she looked up at him with those sweet blue eyes, and he probably would have told her he'd cut off his arm, if that's what she wanted.

"All right. It's a surprise for your mom. I won't breathe a word of it." He hesitated. "Is it her birthday?"

Sorrell didn't seem like she was going to shake her head yes, but Toni stepped forward. "It is. It's her birthday. If you'd like to bring a small gift, that would be nice."

"Toni. You can't ask people to bring gifts," Sorrell said, with a voice that sounded like she was trying to talk under her breath, but she wasn't quite getting there.

He ignored Sorrell. "All right. I'm glad I know. So, I'll expect to come next Tuesday night, and I'll bring a gift for your mom. Will there be other guests?" he asked, and then he figured it would probably be polite for him to offer, so he said, "Should I bring anything else? Something for the meal?"

"Oh no. You don't need to bring anything. We're going to provide it all. And come with a big appetite, because we want you to like it. And eat a lot." Sorrell shot a glance at the other two. Elias wasn't sure what to make of that look, but it made him think they had something planned. Something aside from a birthday meal for their mom.

"All right. Big appetite, gift, and eat a lot. Got it."

"And don't tell anyone," Toni said, giving him a look that made him think that she was going to make a great mom someday.

"No telling anyone. I promise."

"All right. Thanks," Sorrell said, and then she and her friends skipped off, seeming impervious to the cold.

Maybe he'd get used to the temperatures in North Dakota, but half the time, he thought not. Regardless, he smiled as he walked away, looking forward to the Tuesday after next. Hoping he could remember not to say anything to Jane.

Chapter 24

Travis stood with the rest of the football team as the national anthem played.

It was the last football game of the season.

Finally, his senior year, Tadgh had talked him into going out for the team.

He hadn't seen much playing time, warming the bench more than anything else, but he was glad he had done it.

The whole town went nuts over football, and this, the last game of the season, saw more people than he'd seen the entire season.

Everyone in town must have turned out for it.

Keeping his hand over his heart and standing straight, his eyes slanted toward the track that ringed the football field.

Where the cheerleaders stood.

Shanna, in a cropped sweatshirt and tights with her tiny cheerleader skirt barely covering her backside, stood, giggling at something one of the other girls had said.

They'd be in trouble if they talked during the national anthem and the cheerleading coach caught them, but sometimes they got away with a few snide comments. Shanna was supposed to be an assistant coach, but she often seemed to instigate more than teach.

Travis didn't try to bend or break the rules. After seeing his mom, he had determined he would be a rule follower.

Plus, he preferred to do things the right way, rather than slide around, trying to get away with stuff.

He wasn't very good at getting away with things anyway.

Shanna looked good tonight, though. She always did. With her hair in a ponytail and her cheeks red from the cold.

She was the unofficial assistant coach and had made every game.

It's possible that was part of the reason that Travis had gone out for football.

In fact, that was definitely the reason he'd gone out for football.

It hadn't really done him any good. She hadn't noticed him. Of course, he was far from a star player, and that probably had something to do with it.

He'd started too late, and the learning curve was too high. Still, he'd made the team, which was an accomplishment. And he'd seen a little bit of playing time on the offensive line.

He liked to think it was because of his ability and his hard work, and not because the coach felt pity for him.

He wasn't entirely sure about that, but he hoped.

If he were reasonable, he would have shaken his infatuation with Shanna a long time ago, but he couldn't seem to get her out of his head, and she gave him just enough encouragement to keep him coming back. Sometimes he wondered if that was on purpose. She played him like a cat played with a mouse.

The national anthem ended, and the coaches and the captains of the team went out for the coin toss.

He went back to the bench but didn't sit down. He'd get in trouble if he did.

Typically he didn't look at the stands or people or anything while he was playing, trying to keep his focus on the game and what he was supposed to do.

But his eye caught on Ellen as she walked up the track. She was holding something in her jacket, and he couldn't quite make out what it was.

It looked like...a little piglet.

He shook his head. That was Ellen. Always with some kind of animal.

Her bulky jacket and beanie were a far cry from the skimpier outfit that Shanna wore.

Not to mention, Ellen wore boots and what looked like insulated pants. She'd come dressed for the weather.

Which, Travis had to admit, he thought was pretty smart.

He pulled his eyes away from Ellen and the little piglet that she carried in her arms, shaking his head and smiling.

Well, at least he knew that someone would be cheering for him. He and Ellen had developed a bit of a rapport since he walked with her at the parade.

At least, she smiled at him when she saw him, and he did the same.

She was just a little girl, and someday she'd grow up to be a sweet lady.

He turned his eyes back to the field and tried to focus his mind on the game plan for the night.

It was a hard game against their archrival. Brent Stoker, who played tight end, got hurt late in the fourth quarter when they were down by a touchdown.

The crowd groaned as he lay on the ground while Travis looked on, concerned.

He'd seen a little playing time with the offense, more than a few of the other boys who had been sitting on the bench the entire game, but the coach had him sitting this series out.

With Brent's injury, Travis felt a bit of hope stir in his chest.

Tight end was the position that he practiced when he wasn't on the line.

But he hadn't played a single down of that position in any game that season.

So, the hope was small. Although Travis couldn't think of anyone else the coach would put in place of Brent.

So, he paid close attention as the coach came back, once they had gotten Brent up and helped him limp off the field.

"Feagley, you're up."

It took Travis less than half a second to start running to the huddle. He heard Coach tell Steiner, the quarter-back, "Keep the play simple. Take it away from him. Give him time to adjust."

Steiner jerked his head and ran out onto the field behind Travis.

For that series which was three downs and a punt, and the next two offensive plays, all Travis had to do when he was on the field was block.

They were still down by a touchdown and only had a minute and thirty seconds left on the board in the fourth.

The home crowd was yelling, and he could hear the cheerleaders chanting.

He wondered if Shanna had even noticed that he'd gone in. Probably not. She would be leading the cheerleaders, not paying attention to him. Although, they tried to time their chants according to what the team was doing on the field, and someone had to be watching.

So maybe she did know.

Whatever, on the second down, after they had gained zero yardage on a running play, the coach called a passing play that required Travis to block, then get open as the fourth passing option in case none of the other wide receivers had been able to shake their defenders.

Travis did what he was told after the snap, blocking a lineman who was trying to blitz. He spent a few seconds engaged, then shook him and ran over the line of scrimmage.

He turned, shocked to see the ball coming directly toward him.

Maybe if he'd had a dad growing up, maybe if he'd played football with his brothers, maybe if he had done Pee-Wee football, played for years with the team, seeing a football coming toward him would make him do something other than duck.

That was his first instinct, to get out of the way.

His second instinct was to reach up and bat it away.

His third instinct was to catch it.

Thankfully, he had a second and a half to shake off the first and second instinct and snap his hands around the ball.

After that, he turned around and knew what he was supposed to do: run as fast as he could toward the end zone.

He was pretty tough—that was something that he had learned with his brothers and from working on the farm as well.

It was North Dakota, and there were a lot of other boys on both sides of the line who were also farm boy tough.

Still, most of those guys had a dad and hadn't had to scrape and scratch for everything they'd gotten in their lives. Travis figured he was a scrapper, and he was going to take the ball to the end zone, no matter what happened.

He couldn't remember much after that, other than he felt like he'd run so fast he was flying as he went down the field.

He dodged one defender and outran three more, scoring a touchdown with eleven seconds left in the game, and the crowd went crazy.

Travis might have gotten a little nuts too, except he wasn't really used to doing something so big, with so many people watching, and he was more astounded and bemused than celebratory.

It would have been a tie, and they would have gone into overtime, except their kicker was All State, and he made the extra point.

He, Travis Feagley, was the toast of the town, and when the guys who carried him on their shoulders as they left the field set him down, he looked to his left and into the big blue eyes of Shanna Carrolus.

Chapter 25

"It was so good to see you here!" Jane said, giving Brooklyn a big hug. "And I think married life really agrees with you," she added, stepping back and smiling into Brooklyn's eyes.

"Oh, I know it does. It was the best decision of my life," she said, smiling at her husband Cormac, who grinned down at her.

It was crazy that they had been enemies for so many years, and now to look at them looking into each other's eyes like they thought the world of each other...it made Jane's heart smile to see them together and so happy.

"Oh." Brooklyn leaned down and looked around before she said softly, "We'll have a new little one joining us next summer."

"You're kidding!" Jane said, swooping in for another hug, this one tighter and more excited. "That's so amazing. I'm so happy for you."

"We were pretty excited about it too," Brooklyn said, smiling, looking once more at her husband with that soft and endearing look in her eyes that allowed the world to know that she thought he was the best thing that ever happened to her.

Jane smiled with them again and chatted a bit more, knowing that it was too early for them to know the gender, probably too early to even have names picked out. But just basking in the glow of their excitement and newlywed love.

Ten minutes later, she pulled the door closed, flipping the open sign over, sliding the deadbolt, and pulling the shade down once they walked out.

She turned around, leaning against the door and sighing.

"Is it always this crazy on Friday nights?" Elias asked as he walked past the cash register with the empty tub for the dirty dishes in his hand.

"It was the last game of the season. This is the busiest it's ever been, but it's usually crazy. It should settle down after this."

"I know that's bad for business, but I'm happy. Tonight was nuts. And whatever is wrong with Sherry, she couldn't have picked a worse time for it to crop up."

"I know. I don't know how you kept up with everything. It was all I could do to keep up with the orders alongside of Peter." She smiled. "I really appreciate your help and your competence. I would be lost without you."

"God would have sent someone else," he said dismissively.

She grinned, figuring that's what he would say to her compliment. But she meant it. Meant her appreciation, and meant that he was competent.

She'd never worked with anyone that she clicked with better.

"This is the latest we've closed up so far," he commented as he stopped at the first table and cleared up the dishes.

"Yeah. I was only able to take a few minutes to check on the girls and tuck them in bed an hour ago."

"Were they okay?"

"Yes. Neither one of them wanted to go to bed, but with the sickness that's going around, I wanted them to get a good night's rest."

She hoped.

The girls had been helping out, carrying dishes and clearing off tables, and she appreciated it. But while she wanted the diner to be a family affair, she also wanted to make sure that their lives didn't become just working at the diner and nothing else. So she sent them upstairs at seven o'clock to get baths and to have two hours to themselves.

They just about had everything cleaned up when the cow bawl from the other night broke the companionable silence that had descended between Elias and her.

They were both tired and hadn't been talking too much, but it wasn't an awkward silence. It also wasn't the kind of silence where they were just hoping to get home and away from each other.

It was the kind of silence where they were enjoying each other's company without having to say anything

"It's Billy again," Elias said, turning from where he was putting the dirty dishes into the washer.

"Yeah. That's weird."

"We can finish up in here and take an apple out?"

"Yeah. Let's do that," she said, smiling.

It took them another ten minutes, and Billy bawled at least once every minute during that time, but they finally had everything finished up.

Jane grabbed an apple, and then she turned to Elias who waited in the door-way.

"It's your turn to feed him," she said, shrugging into her coat as she walked toward him across the diner.

He already had his coat on, and she'd brought him a beanie out to wear, too. He didn't own one and had been skeptical about wearing one, but he tried it a few times and ended up thanking her for insisting. It made a huge difference in how warm a person was, especially someone who didn't have long hair to help keep the heat in.

"I've never fed a cow before."

"It's not hard. You watched me do it. All you do is put the apple on your hand and hold it out. Remember, he doesn't have teeth on the upper side of his mouth, and if you want to get bitten, you're going to have to work hard at it."

He laughed, remembering that conversation and taking the apple from her. "Are you sure you don't want to?"

"I'm sure."

He unlocked the door and opened it while she walked out.

Billy stood where he had the night before, right in front of the door, looking in like he could see.

"Hey, Billy," she said.

"Billy, this is getting to be a habit. I'm not sure what you're trying to do here, but you really ought to be in bed at this time of night. Don't you know there's a sickness going around?"

Jane laughed at Elias's silliness. "Maybe he doesn't have a mother to tuck him into bed, so he comes here for his midnight snack."

"Billy is too big to have his mother tucking him in. He needs a wife."

Jane grabbed his arm and turned him around.

Careful to keep her face looking serious and trying hard not to laugh at the confused look on his, she motioned with her finger for him to bend over so she could whisper in his ear.

"What?" he asked as he bent down.

"Billy is a steer. That means...he will never get married."

Elias froze for a moment, then his head slowly turned toward hers, and their noses almost touched.

"I take it Billy doesn't know this?" he asked, his breath blowing a cloud around them, their eyes staring into one another.

"He does not," she said, just as serious as she could.

"I feel bad for Billy," he said, which wasn't totally unexpected on her part. But then he said, "Because I think being married would be rather nice."

She wasn't sure what to say about that. She remembered all too well the conversation of the other night when they had been out, and how he explained that he wasn't ready to get married, didn't want to, and wouldn't be anytime soon.

"I don't feel bad for him," she said, her voice low and serious.

"Why not?"

"Because most steers his age are in someone's freezer or on a dinner plate, and instead of that, Billy is standing in front of my diner, about to get an apple. He's a lucky steer."

He had to laugh at that, and they straightened, smiling at each other, just being silly together.

Maybe she would get older and outgrow it, but she hoped not. She hoped she was always ready for a laugh with someone. And for some reason, it was extra special when she got to laugh with Elias.

"I just found some things out about you, son, that made my heart sad. But this crazy woman beside me thinks it's all fun and games. I, on the other hand, commiserate with you, my man," he said, holding the apple out for Billy to sniff.

Billy sniffed the apple immediately, taking it from Elias's hand just as carefully as he'd taken it from Jane's the last time.

Jane went over, rubbing her hands over him again, just checking. "You think I should call Dr. Lark? Just to be sure that there really isn't anything wrong with him?"

"I don't think Dr. Lark can fix what's wrong with him," Elias said.

"Oh my goodness. Are you really that bothered by the information of Billy's lack of a gender?"

"He still has a gender," Elias said.

"So you are. Bothered?"

"Of course. I think any man would be bothered by this."

"No. I think you're wrong. I don't think anyone in town has even given it a thought. It's just what we do with bulls around here."

"All right. I guess I'll try to get used to it. But I still have to feel bad for Billy."

"You go ahead and do that."

"Do they do the same thing with girls?" he asked, coming over and standing beside her where she had stopped at Billy's front shoulder again, scratching his neck like he loved, and behind his horns.

"No. They want cows to have babies. But steers are easier to handle than bulls, plus, after a certain age, bull meat gets stringy. So it's just better off all around if you take care of them when they're younger and easier to handle."

"I see. I was going to ask if it bothered you if they did the same thing to girls, but I guess if they don't, it wouldn't."

She was getting ready to laugh, when he added, "You can't really commiserate, even if you want to have more children someday."

She choked on her laugh.

Did she?

She assumed she was done having children. She'd started rather early and hadn't wanted to be raising kids all her life, as much as she loved her girls.

But as she spent more time with the girls, enjoying them more, she wondered if maybe she might be interested in actually having a family at some point. One with a mom and a dad.

"I...I might. And I can't believe I'm saying that. It scares me a little bit, because I've already been raising two kids by myself. It's no fun. I don't want to be a single mom again, so for me, I guess it's a matter of really deciding whether or not I trust the man I'm with."

"I assume you wouldn't have children with him if you didn't trust him."

"There's the problem." She looked at him, shrugging. "I had every confidence in my husband. I thought he wanted to be with me forever. I was so wrong. What makes me think that I can pick out another one who is actually going to be a good man this time?"

"Did you talk to the Lord about getting married the first time?"

"I wasn't as strong of a Christian back then as I am now. I... I thought I was doing what the Lord wanted me to do. But I wasn't as careful about it, you know? I had more of a tendency to just be like okay, he's going to church, he'll do."

"Rather than actually looking at his character and making sure that everything he said he was actually was what he was when no one was looking?"

"Yes. That exactly."

"So you're smarter now. You can pick out a man who does have character and not be afraid to have children with him."

"I guess you're right. I guess there's a part of me that just gets tired thinking about it though."

"I think having children with the right man wouldn't be nearly as hard as having children with a man who was never around."

"I'm sure you're right. I...love my time with my little girls, but to never have a break, to always be on call, twenty-four hours a day, seven days a week, every meal, every mess, taking them everywhere, grocery shopping, running errands, I mean, just getting a gallon of milk was a major ordeal."

"I can tell from the tone of your voice that the memories aren't that great."

"The memories of my children are amazing, and I love them, but the memories of how hard it was is what gets me. To do that by myself again...no, thank you."

She concentrated on petting Billy for a moment, and then she turned to him.

"Would you be interested in having children?" she asked, hoping it didn't sound like she was asking for herself. She had been as honest with him as she could. Even though she knew they weren't really planning on going anywhere with their relationship. They were just out here as friends. Even though it felt a little bit more intimate than that to her.

"Yeah. I've never been around kids much in my life, never been super interested in them. But just being around them in the diner here and seeing your girls, who I really like, by the way, and are pretty awesome kids, I guess… I guess I wouldn't mind. Which is kind of weird because it's really not something I've thought about."

She nodded, not saying anything.

"But I suppose that's something I have to leave in God's hands. After all, the choice to have children really isn't mine. As much as I like to think I'm in charge of every aspect of my life, I'm really not. The older I get, the more I realize that."

"Same. Although, I guess having my husband walk out on me was a good lesson in learning that I'm not in charge of every aspect of my life, and I can't control the people around me. I can only control myself."

Chapter 26

Jane didn't want to dredge up old memories every time they talked. She wanted that part of her life to be over. And it really was, although she could still at times feel the pain and fear and total hopelessness she felt when her ex had left.

She was opening her mouth to change the subject when Billy pushed her again.

When she first stood beside him, she kind of wondered if he might not like her and might push her again as he had before.

Although different people in the diner had mentioned that they thought Billy was a matchmaking steer, which she had laughed about.

She figured he was a clumsy steer, or one who lost his balance, or one who enjoyed keeping people on their toes.

She'd been prepared for a nudge. But after coming out and talking to Elias for a while, she had fallen into their easy camaraderie and had been thinking a lot about what he'd said. She'd totally forgotten to be on guard for any kind of maneuver on Billy's part.

Therefore, he totally caught her off guard, and she stumbled back.

This time, Elias must have been caught off guard as well, because he stumbled back also, even though his arms went around her.

His foot caught on the crack of the sidewalk, and they both landed heavily on the cement walk.

"There aren't too many times in my life where I wished for snow, but a foot of snow would have made that landing a lot softer," Jane said, smarting from landing on her elbow and hip. At least her head hadn't smacked the sidewalk. She twisted. "Are you okay?"

"I'm good. I didn't hit my head, so that's good. I tried to twist so I was taking the fall but didn't quite make it the whole way around."

"You took the brunt of it, although my hip hurts."

He grunted. "If I didn't know any better, I'd think that steer did it on purpose. That he actually tried to knock you over the last time we were out here."

"Haven't you heard the rumors around town about the steer?" she asked, letting the throbbing pain in her elbow subside before she tried to get up. It was dark, the streets were deserted, and no one was watching. It wasn't like she had to scramble up to get out of anyone's way.

"No. What rumors?"

"You're a waiter. You should know every rumor in this town."

"I don't usually pay attention to those kinds of things. I listen to the weather forecast about the first hour that I'm on, and then I tune that out too. That's all people seem to talk about around here, the weather."

"They do talk about that a lot," she acknowledged. "But they also talk about Billy and his penchant for pushing couples together. I've heard a few people calling him Billy the lover boy, which I didn't think to tell you back when we were talking about the fact that he's a steer."

"Shh! Don't let him hear you say that. You said he doesn't know."

"Are you seriously joking?"

"I kinda am. Yeah."

"Then you must not be hurt very badly."

"No, I'm not. I...I'm kind of enjoying this."

"Lying on the sidewalk?" she asked, turning until she was completely facing him, leaning on her elbow, but intending to get up.

"No. Lying beside you."

"Lying beside me, on the sidewalk?" she emphasized the on the sidewalk part.

"Well, if I could have chosen some-where, this probably wouldn't have been my first choice. But since Billy seems to have chosen for us, and you're not mov-ing, I decided I was going to enjoy it."

"I can move," she said, scrambling to get up.

His arms came around her, and he said, "That wasn't a hint."

"Are you sure I'm not pushing you into anything?" she asked, knowing she really wasn't on him much at all, since she just rolled over and lay beside him, looking at him.

Maybe their legs were a little tangled together.

"No." He grinned. "I can see the head-line now—they found us out here, frozen, lying on the sidewalk in front of the diner door."

"With Billy standing over the top of us? They would probably have some very good ideas of what Billy was up to," she said, sounding a little bit amused, but she also knew that they didn't want those kinds of rumors flying around town about them. Especially since they weren't true. "Remember, it's a small town, and if we get people talking like that about us, it's going to be a hard thing to live down."

"I'll keep that in mind," he said, almost sounding like he didn't care, but he didn't say that. Maybe both of them were thinking about their previous conversation and how neither one of them was looking for marriage, and so neither one of them wanted to have a relationship, when they couldn't put everything they were into it.

"On that note, we'd better get up."

"Let me go first, and I'll give you a hand. Not because you can't do it," he said, looking at her like she was going to protest. "But because I want to."

"All right." It didn't take any time at all for him to get up, and he gave her hand.

They gave Billy one last pat, then Elias opened the diner door, and they went in, locking it behind them.

"I feel like Billy is going to be making a habit of that," he said, and he sounded thoughtful.

"What do you mean?" Jane asked.

"If the townspeople are right, and he is a matchmaking steer, then he's probably not going to leave us alone until we do what he wants us to do."

"I see." She wasn't sure what to think about that. And she supposed he probably wasn't either.

"It's late. You're tired. I'm thinking about what we talked about last time and not sure that I still mean everything I said. I might want to change my mind."

"You're right," she said as they walked through the diner, past the cash register, and into the kitchen. She looked around, noting that everything was in its place, and she walked through, noting that Elias turned out the lights as he exited the room. "I'm tired. And I don't want to think."

She had thought she had everything all figured out. She hadn't wanted to have a relationship, hadn't wanted to even think about marriage, had been focused on the diner. But maybe spending time with Elias and having him step into the picture, maybe she wasn't sure exactly what she really wanted after all.

Once the kitchen light was out, it was dark with just a little light coming in through the window of the door. One of the girls must have left her boots on the floor, because as Jane turned to wish Elias good night, she tripped.

She didn't exactly fall into his arms, but she took a bigger step forward than she had meant to take, and she ended up bumping into him. His arms came around her, and her hands landed on his chest.

Maybe that wasn't a very good excuse, but her head lifted, and the next thing she knew, his head descended toward hers, and their lips met.

She certainly hadn't planned that and knew he hadn't either, but she didn't do too much thinking, because her mouth softened under his and the kiss deepened and her hands which had been on his chest slid around his neck and shoulders, pulling him closer, while his tightened around her waist, pressing her to him, and maybe it was the dark, or maybe it was the cold, or maybe it was what she had been thinking, but her heart beat hard and her breath caught and it felt like it was just the two of them in the world, together, and she didn't want the kiss to ever end.

But he pulled back eventually, or maybe she did, because she had to breathe, and they stood in the dark, her looking up, trying to see his eyes but unable to because of the darkness and not even able to make out anything but the dim shadow of his lips. They were parted, he needed to suck in air or maybe was dealing with surprise. His hands never loosened their grip on her.

She liked being held tightly, liked the idea that someone didn't want to let her go. That she was worth that much to someone. But she knew, from experience, that the physical aspect could be deceiving.

He might not want to let her go until he got what he wanted out of her.

Except, it was Elias, and she didn't think he was like that.

"I didn't mean to do that," he whispered.

"I didn't either."

"I don't exactly want to take it back, but I definitely don't want to make things awkward between us either. And I'm afraid that might."

"Yeah. That was my fear too."

They had to work together. He would wait tables in the morning. They would be in the kitchen together. Would they still have the same easy banter?

"I won't tell you to forget about it, because I know I won't, but maybe we can just think about it for a little bit?" he asked, his words uncertain, like he wasn't sure exactly what he was saying.

She got it. He didn't want a relationship. He wanted the kissing but not the relationship. And when she threw herself at him, he was going to kiss her but still wasn't going to want a relationship.

It wasn't like she hadn't been married before.

The thought made her sad, but it also didn't surprise her. She'd already warned herself not to get wrapped up in him. Warned herself not to allow herself to get her feelings so entangled that she would be hurt when he left.

"That's a good idea to me," she said, trying to disentangle herself from him.

"Wait."

She froze but stayed stiff. She wasn't going to melt against him, when he was just going to tell her that he didn't want a relationship.

"You're tense. You're quiet, and you're upset with me."

"No. I'm upset with myself. Sometimes I'm just stupid." She pulled away, and this time, he let her go.

"You're not stupid," he said a little louder because she had turned up the stairs.

"No, you don't know what I've done," she said softly, thinking about how she'd pretty much fallen for him and known the whole time she shouldn't have. Now her emotions were involved. It was going to be impossible for her to make a rational decision, especially if the decision necessitated her overwriting her emotions in order to carry it out.

"What you've done?" he asked, obviously not understanding.

And she was not going to enlighten him. He didn't need to know the extent of her feelings. And she wasn't going to bare her heart to someone who was going to end up being someone else's husband.

"Good night," she said, turning and walking up the stairs.

"Jane. I don't understand."

"We can talk tomorrow about tonight. I promise, if you want to, we can talk about it sometime, but not tonight."

"Are we still friends?" he called as she reached the top of the stairs.

"Yes. I would never think of saying we weren't friends, just because I did something stupid."

"Are you sure it was you and not me?"

"I'm sure."

"Good night, Jane," he said softly, his words barely carrying up to her. He sounded sad. And she felt bad about it, but there wasn't anything she could do. He probably wasn't going to understand, and although she'd promised to talk to him, she could hardly explain that she'd fallen in love with him, stupidly, because she knew he didn't want to get married.

She'd done everything she always hoped to do. Had made sure that the man that she was with had character and integrity and was honest and caring. She also knew that he was loyal and hardworking.

But the one thing she hadn't really been thinking about hadn't happened.

He also had to want to have a relationship with her. A relationship that involved more than hanging out together or making out. That's not what she wanted for the next twenty years of her life. Some man who didn't want to make a commitment to marriage but just wanted her as his girlfriend to make out with on occasion.

She wasn't going to be one of those girls who sat around for years waiting for some man to be ready to propose.

Elias might be worth it, but he didn't want her enough to take that step.

And that's where she'd messed up.

Chapter 27

Why had he gone and done something so stupid?

Elias couldn't believe how dumb he had been.

What had he been thinking?

Obviously he wasn't thinking. He hadn't been able to think well when he was around Jane for a while now. But that was the first time he'd completely lost his head.

He'd just told her not that long ago he didn't kiss girls he wasn't intending to marry.

And yet, he went and kissed her.

Now, she walked away because she hadn't wanted a relationship, and she knew he only kissed girls he wanted to marry.

It was his policy.

And his policy hadn't changed.

He hadn't come to Sweet Water intending to get married. And he wasn't in any better position to be a husband or father than he was back when he told Jane.

The only difference was, he felt like if he and Jane were together, they could make it work.

But obviously, she hadn't changed her mind about what she'd said, and his kiss had scared her.

He'd worked all morning without her saying more than ten words to him.

None of them had been unnecessary words. Except for the good morning that she greeted him with, subdued and much quieter than her normal happy greeting.

The dark circles around her eyes said that she probably hadn't slept any better than he had the night before.

He wanted to talk to her. Wanted to tell her that he didn't mean it. Except, that wouldn't be true. He couldn't take it back. Couldn't tell her that he didn't have the absolutely most honorable intentions possible.

So what was he going to do?

He didn't know. He did manage to make it through the breakfast brunch and lunch rush, which on Saturdays often blended together, but they had a lull in the middle of the afternoon.

It was two o'clock, and only one man sat at a table in the corner of the diner.

Elias only knew him as Preacher but figured he had a regular name. He was one of the Stryker brothers, and typically if he came in, he came in with his wife and children.

There seemed to be a bunch of Stryker men with families, but this man was alone today.

He had his lunch on one side and his Bible open on the other.

Elias couldn't help but notice the Bible was splattered, dirty, and well-worn, like the man took it with him everywhere.

He'd heard about Preacher's wisdom and how he usually gave good advice, and because there was no one else in the diner, and Jane was avoiding him, he'd been tempted to go over and strike up a conversation.

Except he didn't know what to say. But he did walk over five minutes after he delivered the man's food and ask how his meal was.

"Good. It always is here." The man smiled, gentle and mild. His eyes held such acceptance and love that it took Elias aback. He had never seen that kind of deep emotion in any man before. But Preacher was definitely different. In a lot of ways.

"You need me to fill up your drink?" he asked, nodding to the empty coffee cup.

"No, thank you," the man said. "One coffee is enough." He paused, and then his eyes narrowed. "Looks like you got something on your mind, son. Want to talk about it?"

Even though Preacher had some young, school-age children, Elias figured he was probably ten or fifteen years older than he was.

He wasn't going to ask, but since the invitation had been issued, he nodded his head and slid into the booth across from Preacher.

Preacher was one of those men who didn't seem to need to fill out the silence with a bunch of talk. He simply sat, chewing thoughtfully, his face open, waiting.

It gave Elias the time he needed to think about what he wanted to say.

"I'm sorry. I know you don't know me from anyone else."

"I've heard about you. Small town." Preacher gave a small grin.

"Yeah. So then maybe you know I'm ex-military."

"Yes. Heard some rumors about that."

"My dishonorable discharge?"

Preacher inclined his head but didn't say anything.

"I came here to basically pick up the pieces. I didn't want to come, really. I had a career in mind, but that blew up in my face. Spent all of my money on the farm

I bought with my buddies here, and it just seemed like the wisest course of action was to come here and... I don't even know. I'm not that interested in running it. And they're doing well without me."

"You might be able to deed off a piece and build a house," Preacher suggested.

"Yeah, I guess I'd thought about that. The farm actually is four different plots put together. But..."

"But there's something else?"

"Yeah. There's..."

"Jane?"

"How'd you know?" Elias asked. He wasn't going to say Jane's name. He was going to just mention that there was a girl.

"Well, I have my wife, Reina, to thank for that. I'm not always very astute in that regard. But she suggested that maybe Jane had feelings for you, and it seemed to me, once she said it, that you had feelings for her too."

It wasn't a question. Preacher wasn't interrogating him, but he was asking gently, in a way that felt nonthreatening, and Elias nodded.

"I do."

"You don't seem like the kind of man that usually has trouble making a decision."

"I didn't used to be. But I guess whenever everything you have planned kind of crumbles around your ears, you have a tendency to question yourself. Ques-

tion your work, your life, question everything."

"And it's hard to get the confidence
back once you've lost it."

"Yeah."

"You're not any less in God's eyes than
you were before that happened."

Elias nodded. Preacher's words were
simple, but they felt a little profound.
God didn't think any less of him because
of what happened. God still loved him
the exact same amount. God still cared
for him exactly the same.

Maybe even more, since he felt more
needy than he had been before.

"I think, sometimes it's hard for a confident man or, even worse, an arrogant
man to let God lead. Sometimes God

needs to knock us off our pedestals before we can turn to Him and truly humble ourselves, and submit to whatever His will is."

"You know, I was thinking that same thing. That all of the things I thought were terrible, God was working out for my good. I suppose that's just one more thing. He needed to humble me so that I would be more willing to listen."

"To move to a small town in the middle of nowhere. One where the climate is not exactly hospitable?" Preacher said with humor lacing his tone, although his eyes still held compassion.

"Yeah. I definitely wouldn't have come to Sweet Water on my own."

"Only God could get you to do that."

"That's true."

"I wonder what God wanted you to do in this town?" Preacher said thoughtfully, like he was truly asking the question. Just wondering.

That took Elias aback. He hadn't considered God would have a plan for him in this town.

"I don't know," he murmured, but he was still thinking.

"You don't think it's on the ranch?" Preacher asked, prompting him.

He wasn't the slightest bit interested in ranching. "Would God lead me to something I don't have any interest in or aptitude for?"

Preacher laughed. "Maybe. Sometimes God does. Sometimes He points us in a direction that we would never have said that we could go. If you've ever read the book, The Hiding Place, that author was a watch repair woman. Very humble and unassuming. She ended up being part of the resistance in Holland. She wasn't fit for that kind of work, she didn't have the aptitude for it, but she had the location, and God equipped her with the aptitude when she needed it."

"Interesting. So you think He might give me an aptitude and ability to ranch?"

He hated to admit how very terrible he was. He hadn't even known that Billy was a steer, which meant that, well, anyway, he wasn't going to be a husband. Which seemed like a very elementary way to explain it. And he was way too embarrassed to say that to Preacher, even though he had a good idea that Preacher wouldn't laugh at him.

"I'm not saying that. I'm asking. God isn't going to tell me what you're supposed to do." Preacher looked at his Bible. It was a fond glance. "But you can often find the answers in God's word. Sometimes going to a counselor will help you straighten out your thinking. Make it fall in line with the Word of God."

"I guess that's why I sat down here beside you. I saw the Bible, and it's not every day you see a man sitting in here with his Bible opened, so I figured you wouldn't steer me wrong. Even if you couldn't tell me what I need to do."

"If only life were that simple, right? Just tell me what to do, and I'll do it."

"Yeah."

He kept thinking—God had led him to the small town. Someplace he would never have come.

"And what happened to you once you got here?" Preacher asked, continuing his line of questioning.

"I ended up with a job I wasn't expecting," Elias said without thinking.

"This job?" Preacher asked, although he probably knew the answer.

"Yeah."

"Do you think that was the Lord?"

"It had to be. There's no way I would have asked to be a waiter..." His words faded off. He wouldn't have asked to be a waiter. Would never have thought to work here. He wouldn't have gotten to know Jane. He wouldn't have realized that being a server wasn't something he hated. That working in the diner wasn't a bad life. That... It might be small, but there were plenty of opportunities for growth.

Had God led him to North Dakota so that he could meet Jane, her children, and marry her, settle down, working in the diner with her?

Now that was a life plan he had not seen coming.

It could only be from the Lord, if that was the way he was supposed to go. It certainly wasn't a plan he would have thought about in high school, college, or in the military, or last month, even.

"Because it looks to me like you might be figuring out some answers..." Preacher allowed room for him to fill in if he wanted to.

"I am, but I messed up."

"Join the club," Preacher said.

"No. I mean big time."

Preacher nodded but didn't say anything, his position inviting Elias to talk if he wanted to.

Elias mentioned his conversation with Jane, how he said that he didn't plan on kissing anyone unless he was planning on marrying her. Then he kissed her and upset her.

"The only thing I can figure is..." He looked over toward the kitchen area, which was partially hidden behind the counter and a half wall. Jane wasn't in sight. "She decided that I wanted to marry her, and that scared her to death. And she pulled away and doesn't want to have anything to do with me, sending me a clear signal that she doesn't want to get married."

"Did she kiss you back?"

"Yeah." Elias gave him a look. "I wouldn't have kissed her otherwise."

"Just asking. I feel like Jane isn't the kind of girl who goes around just kissing anyone."

"She's not."

"Did she tell you that she wasn't?"

"She said the same thing I did. That she believed it wasn't right to kiss people you weren't intending to marry. Like I know that the world thinks kissing is just kind of a throwaway thing you can do with anyone, but...that just seems...like the wrong kind of thinking."

"So, might she be thinking the same thing you want?" Preacher asked.

Elias froze. It stumped him for a minute, having never considered that idea, but the more he thought about it, the more he realized...maybe she was.

"I guess she could be. We kind of fell into it, and I wouldn't say that I kissed her necessarily, as much as we kissed each other."

"Just an idea. But also, maybe she's pulling away from you because she knows you don't want a relationship, and possibly, it scares her that she knows you don't, and she thinks that kiss was just an accident. Which it was. And she's figured out that she doesn't want it to be an accident. But she thinks you aren't interested in anything more." Preacher raised his shoulder. "It's kind of hard to tell, and there could even be something else. But I wouldn't just come to a conclusion and assume that you're right. I know it's really hard to convince yourself that what you think you know isn't the most accurate version of the truth. But sometimes it's not."

Elias knew that, but he had never quite articulated it like that before. Preacher had a way with words, a way of saying things that made him see more clearly.

And he could be right. Maybe Jane wasn't pulling away from him because she hated him or didn't want to have anything to do with him. Maybe she was pulling away for something completely different. Something that he didn't know, or something that Preacher had suggested.

"Thank you. Sometimes it just helps to get a different perspective. I hadn't thought about things like that before." He took another glance over and still didn't see Jane. He appreciated the fact that the diner had stayed empty, because he couldn't have had this conversation with anyone else near enough to hear.

"What do you think I should do?" he finally asked, feeling about as humble as he'd ever felt in his life before.

Normally it was his job to tell people what to do. He made the decisions. He gave the orders. Of course, he had to follow the orders that came down from his higher-ups, but he was still a commander. Still a leader.

This was a new experience and one he hadn't felt for a really long time.

His heart sank when Preacher shook his head.

"I wish I could tell you what to do. That would make life a lot easier, wouldn't it?"

"Yeah." They'd already talked about that. And he should have known Preacher wasn't going to offer.

"I guess I would just say don't rush into anything. Either running away or running toward her. Just relax and let her know you're still her friend. And if she tries not to talk to you, you don't have to give up on that. You can keep saying things, asking her questions, teasing information out of her. Can't you?"

"I'm not a great conversationalist. I'm not exactly known for my ability to talk about anything, but it always seemed easy to talk to Jane."

"Usually it does with the woman you love," Preacher said with a little smile.

Like he knew exactly what Elias was talking about.

Except Elias hadn't really considered that he loved Jane.

Did he?

The bells over the door jingled, and a blast of cold air came in as Mav, Preacher's brother, and his wife, Cassie, came in.

"I'll get out of here, in case your brother wants to sit down with you," Elias said after looking around to see Mav.

"Hey there, guys," Mav said, holding his hand out to shake with Elias. Preacher stood, shaking his hand as well and nodding at Cassie.

They sat down in the seat Elias just vacated, and Elias took their drink orders before heading to the back to get them.

Preacher had given him a lot to think about. And probably the best advice was to not run away, to not rush into anything. Just be a friend. Be a friend, until God presented the opportunity for more.

So, he set about doing that for the rest of the day, just smiling at Jane and working to have their usual easy conversation.

She was chilly at first, but by the end of the day, while he didn't feel like he'd made significant progress, he felt like he'd made enough to say that Preacher was right. At the very least, they could get their friendship back. It was up to him to work on it if that's what he wanted. He couldn't just walk away when things got hard. Or give up when he ran into something he wasn't expecting.

If he wanted Jane, he might have to risk his heart for her. But at the very least, he was going to risk his pride and try to win her friendship back.

Chapter 28

Tuesday evening, Elias showed up at the back door of the diner, a small gift in hand, wearing a brand-new pair of cowboy boots, which hurt his feet, new jeans, and a button-down shirt like the rest of the men around town wore.

He had eschewed the belt buckle that usually went with such ensembles, but he had broken down and bought a cow-boy hat.

Jonah and Gideon had insisted it was worth the money. They said it would last and he would wear it for years. He'd taken their word for it but felt a little con-spicuous as he stood at the back door.

It wasn't locked, so he walked in, grate-ful to get out of the cold. He wore a sheepskin jacket, but he hadn't put his beanie hat on under his cowboy hat.

The guys had said he could, but while this wasn't exactly a date, he did want to make a good impression, and he wasn't sure exactly that a beanie hat was saying what he was trying to impart to Jane.

Ha. He wasn't exactly sure what he was trying to impart. That he was serious about marrying her? That she could take a chance on him? That he would wait until she was ready?

He wasn't sure. But he was going to embrace it. Because he figured out one thing. God might have brought him to North Dakota against his will, but He had a purpose in mind, and Elias was almost certain that that purpose had to do with Jane.

The diner came second, but Jane and her girls stood out to him as the whole reason that everything up to that point had happened in his life. Maybe he was wrong. It seemed like a huge leap of faith, since the woman that he was pretty sure God had destroyed his military career for, and moved him to a town in the middle of nowhere, and had him working as a waiter for, was barely talking to him.

The last few days, he'd tried to do just as Preacher had said and simply be a friend.

They still didn't have their easy friendship back, and when Billy had bawled outside the diner door, instead of going out, Jane had said that Lark had checked him out and said he was fine.

She had handed him an apple and said he could take it out if he wanted to.

Feeling bad for the steer, feeling even worse that the woman that he was fairly certain he was supposed to marry didn't want to have anything to do with him, he had gone out and commiserated with Billy for a little while.

He hoped the steer felt better, although Billy did seem a little sad that Jane wasn't there.

Maybe that was whimsical thinking, but that was the way he had felt when he had been petting him.

Regardless, tonight he'd show up for her birthday. He had gotten her something small, not wanting to be extravagant or get anything too personal. He didn't want to scare her off even more than what she already was. But it was thoughtful enough that he hoped she understood that she meant a lot to him, and he would do everything in his power to take care of her, protect her, love her. Cherish her.

His palms sweated, and he resisted the urge to wipe them against the legs of his jeans, holding the gift with his fingertips so he wouldn't smudge the paper.

Taking a breath, realizing it had been a long time since he'd been this nervous, a very long time, he knocked on the apartment door at the top of the steps.

What was the worst that could happen? She could tell him she never wanted to see him again. And he'd survive.

He didn't want that to happen, but he tried to calm his nerves by reminding himself that God was in charge and that he was just doing what he thought he was supposed to.

Of course, he wanted to do it too. And that maybe muddied the waters just a bit. Because sometimes he got confused with what he wanted and what God wanted. He was pretty sure they were one and the same in this instance though.

"Hey, Mr. Elias." Merritt opened the door. "You're early."

"I didn't want to be late," he said. But he knew he had a tendency to be early.

"Mom's not home yet."

"Oh? Where's she?" He didn't mean to ask like that, but she'd surprised him.

"She's supposed to be going to get her hair and nails done," Sorrell said, from where she stood over the stove. "She didn't want to, but we made her."

"I see. Why didn't she want to?"

"She said she'd rather sit in the back of the church and talk to the Lord for a little while, but we said this was a special occasion, and we wanted her to look nice."

"I see. So did she promise that she would go?"

The girls looked at each other. They tilted their heads, as though trying to remember whether their mom had said she would actually do what they wanted her to do or not.

"I don't know?"

He was tempted to go to the church, just to see if she was there, because he could see Jane wanting the peace and quiet. And maybe being as conflicted as he was.

Of course, he could also see her doing what her girls wanted her to do, just to make them happy.

"Can I do something to help?" he asked, looking at the stove and feeling a little bit more comfortable about his cooking abilities now that he'd been working in a diner for a few weeks.

"Nope. We've got it all under control. You can go sit down at the table, and as soon as Mom is here, we should be ready."

"Aren't you girls sitting with me?" he said, walking to the kitchen table.

"No. Not that table. We're going to serve you in the other room, where the card table is set up. Only, we put a tablecloth over it so it doesn't look like a card table anymore. Be careful with the candle," Sorrell said.

He grinned at the girls. They were sweet. Just like their mom. And he felt a stirring in his chest. Maybe a bit of protectiveness, a feeling that he wanted them to be a part of his family.

"All right. I'll watch the candle," he said, like he wasn't thirty-something years old and knowledgeable about not wanting to start fires.

He wandered into the room, which was cozy but small. The girls had decorated nicely, with a tablecloth over a card table, fancy in Elias's opinion, and a fancy dinnerware set—two spoons and two forks and all the fancy things that a person might find at an upscale restaurant.

He didn't want to ask, but he bet they looked up online how to place all of them.

It was sweet. Then he realized that the table was only set up for two, and that must mean that they intended for him to eat with their mom...alone.

"Hey, girls? Aren't you guys eating with us at all?"

"No. We're getting it ready, then we're going over to Toni's house. We have some things we need to do over there."

"You're not hungry?"

"No. But you are, aren't you?" Sorrell popped her head around the doorway and looked at him.

"Yeah. I'm starving. You guys told me to come hungry, so I haven't eaten all day."

Part of that was nerves, but he didn't tell them.

That wasn't something he would admit to just anyone.

He sat down, but fidgeted, so got up and went over to look out the window. He stood staring out at the street when he heard the door open and Jane's voice.

"Oh my goodness. It smells so good in here! You guys are amazing. I hope it tastes as good as it smells."

"I think it will, Mom. You didn't eat anything while you were out, did you?" Sorrell asked.

Before Jane could answer, Merritt said, "Mom! Your hair is gorgeous. They must have been able to do makeup at the shop."

"They did. So I had it all done. I even got my nails done."

There was silence, then the girls said, "Wow. Those are beautiful."

Jane sounded perky and happy and everything he wanted her to be.

But he wanted her to be that when she saw him.

Maybe she hadn't seen his Jeep, since he parked in front.

He set the gift down on the mantel and walked over to the doorway.

Jane wore some kind of swishy skirt that ruffled around her legs, and the boots she wore were more stylish than functional, making her something that he might have heard other women call cute.

Her blouse flowed, and the girls were right. He had hardly ever seen her with anything but her hair pulled up in a scrunchy or even a tight bun, and now it flowed around her shoulders to the middle of her back.

He had no idea what she got done with it, but it was pretty. Beautiful.

It made him want to touch it.

She turned around, as though she were going to walk into the living room, maybe to take her things somewhere, and she froze when she saw him.

He'd never seen her with makeup on, and while he thought he liked the regular Jane better, he had to admit this Jane was pretty darn nice, too.

Beautiful. So beautiful.

Her hand flew to her chest. "Elias?"

"Happy birthday," he said.

That made her blink. "It's not my birthday."

With her brows drawn, she looked at her girls. Both of them looked guilty.

"We told him it was your birthday, because we wanted him to come for your birthday party dinner."

"We didn't really celebrate your birthday, so we thought today would be the day."

Jane's eyes narrowed, and she put a hand on her hip, but she didn't seem angry, just...he wasn't sure.

Finally, she said in a tone that held no censure, just parental wisdom, "If you're going to tell someone that we're having a birthday party for someone, it's probably best to tell them that it's not their actual birthday. That way they're not confused. Because that's skirting on the edge of lying, and we don't want to be known as liars. Once you get that reputation, it's hard to shake."

The girls both nodded, and that seemed to be all Jane was going to say about it.

She turned back around, more composed now. He liked the flustered and shocked Jane better. He'd seen more of what he wanted to see in her eyes at that point.

"I'm sorry you thought it was my birthday," she said coolly.

"I'm not." He wasn't here to celebrate her birthday, so he would happily take a makeup day. "When is your actual birthday?"

"It's in April."

"This is your half birthday?"

She scrunched her face up and seemed to think about it. "I guess it is. It's the exact day."

"I'll remember that," he said, making a mental note to go home and write it down. He would never remember if he didn't, but he didn't want to forget.

He would guess, as a single mom, she probably hadn't had too many people helping her celebrate her birthdays over the years, and he wanted that to change, if she was going to be with him. Even if they were just going to be friends, friends helped friends celebrate birthdays, right?

"Mom. Sit down," Sorrell commanded from behind Jane in the doorway.

"Okay. Sorry," she said, walking over to the table. "Is there a certain seat that's mine?"

"No. Just pick one, Mr. Elias, you need to sit down too." Sorrell didn't give him any room for argument, not that he wanted to. He walked to the same side Jane did, and when she gave him a look, he pulled her chair out for her.

She seemed like she might have been charmed by that, because she almost smiled. She did murmur, "Thank you," as she settled herself down.

He walked around and took his own seat.

"I just want you to know that I didn't have anything to do with this."

"I believe you. I'm not sure what the girls are up to, but I believe you."

"You think they're up to something?"

"Sure. I'm positive. I'm just not sure what it is."

They didn't have any more time to talk, because the girls came marching into the room, setting containers down on the table.

A container of roasted Brussels sprouts, which Elias wasn't sure he even liked, a container of corn, and a container that was covered. There was a small white card that was folded over the top of the container, and as the girl set it down on the table, he read the card.

Marry Me Chicken.

"Aren't you girls going to eat?" Jane asked.

"No, we have to go to Toni's house. She's expecting us, and we have some things to do. Her mom said she would check in with you later."

"Her mom knows you're going to her house?"

"Yeah. We got permission, Mom."

"Okay," Jane said, a little uncertainly.

The girls didn't waste any time, but turned the lights off in the kitchen, and ran out the door, their feet thundering on the steps. Their coats and boots and hats were down beside the back door.

Almost by mutual agreement, neither one of them said anything.

Chapter 29

The whole time her daughters were bustling around, Jane was squirming inside. She wasn't sure when she had been more embarrassed in her life before.

If there was ever a time for a trapdoor to open underneath her and drop her through the ceiling, this would be the time.

Lord?

Nothing happened. Then the door slammed, and there was silence in the apartment.

Jane couldn't tear her eyes away from that little piece of cardboard on top of the covered dish.

Marry Me Chicken.

Finally, without lifting her eyes from the cardboard sign, she said, "I promise you, on a stack of Bibles if you want me to, I promise, I did not put my girls up to this."

The words came from deep inside of her, pulled out almost raggedly, because she wanted so badly for him to believe her.

But why would he?

It seemed like such an obvious happening. He'd kissed her. He said he only kissed people he was expecting to marry, and then when he tried to make friendly overtures and remind her that they were just friends, she hadn't been the least bit welcoming or warm.

She'd been trying to protect her heart by not being kind to him, but the result was the same.

It hadn't helped their relationship at all, and they hadn't figured anything out.

"Why would I think that?" he asked, after what felt like a million years had passed.

Her eyes slipped from the card and flew to his.

Did he mean it? Did he really not think she did this on purpose? Made up her birthday, went and got her hair and nails done, she was even wearing makeup and a skirt for goodness' sake, and the dish was Marry Me Chicken.

It was crazy. What else could he think?

"Why wouldn't you?" was the only thing she could think to say.

"I can't think of any reasons why I would. I thought your daughters were celebrating your birthday. I thought we were having a meal with all of us, but it looks like they left. I am not sure what has you so upset, but your cheeks are on fire, and even the tips of your ears are pink."

Before she could stop it, her hand went up to touch her ear. Like that would confirm whether or not it was actually pink.

He huffed out a laugh. "Why? What has you so...upset?"

"I just thought you would have thought I set this up. That you would think that since you kissed me, I thought that you were going to marry me. And all of this," she ran her hand up and down herself, indicating her makeup and her hair and nails and dress, "everything set up like I'm reminding you that you're supposed to marry me now that you kissed me. I didn't think anything of the kind. In fact, I honestly thought the opposite."

"The opposite?"

"That you regretted it. That you didn't want it to happen again. You don't want a relationship. You told me that. I heard you. I promise I wasn't trying to push you into anything."

"All right. I think there's just a lot of mis-understanding between us. But while we're straightening this out, the food is getting cold. So, I think we need to pray, and then I think we ought to eat and we ought to talk." He moved a little, bending his head down to try to meet her eyes.

Chapter 30

Jane looked at Elias, still embarrassed but knowing he was right.

"Does that sound okay to you?"

"It sounds very reasonable. It sounds like something adults would do, instead of the way I've been acting, which is rather childish, and I'm sorry. I... I was scared."

"Let's get something straight between us. You don't have to be scared. Okay?"

He didn't understand. He didn't know that he had the power to hurt her. And that's what made her scared.

But she just pulled back, didn't say anything, and then bowed her head and waited for him to pray.

"Father God, we thank You for this food. And I thank You for the woman across the table from me. I pray that You'll bless our conversation, help me to have the words to say to let her know how much I love her, and please, help her come to her senses and agree to marry me. In Jesus's name, amen."

Jane's head snapped up long before he said amen.

His head lifted slower, and he met her eyes over the table.

"You shouldn't pray things you don't mean," she said immediately, not sure why, but she felt angry. Like he was messing with her, and she didn't appreciate it. Her feelings weren't things to be trifled with.

"I meant that with my whole heart."

Those words took the wind right out of her sails.

"You meant it?" she asked, knowing her voice held a lot of skepticism.

"Would you like some corn?" he asked, reaching for the bowl.

"No thank you." She paused. "You really meant it?"

"I told you I did," he said, putting a spoonful of corn on his plate. "Would you like some of these things?"

"They're roasted Brussels sprouts."

"I was afraid of that."

She snorted. She couldn't help it. "Yes. I'll take some." She didn't think she could eat. Her stomach felt like a tight ball of cement, just stuck to her backbone. But he was right. They needed to act like adults, and her girls had worked hard to put this together. "Normally I don't have to talk myself into acting like an adult."

"No. I've worked with you for a while now, and I've never seen you act anything less than gracious and kind."

"I haven't been very kind to you this week."

"That's the only exception."

"It's kind of a big one."

"I'll give you grace for it."

"Really?"

"You seem to be questioning me an awful lot tonight. Is there a reason for that?" he asked, letting humor show in his eyes, so she knew that he wasn't really serious, that he was just messing with her.

"You seem to be saying an awful lot of things that are really hard to believe," she returned, putting some Brussels sprouts on her plate, then putting the spoon for the Brussels sprouts back in the bowl.

"Should we try this?" he asked, lifting a brow at the Marry Me Chicken.

"I don't know. What do you think?" She eyed the container. "It could be sketchy stuff."

"Or it could be good enough to ease your mind and make you a little more receptive when I try to kiss you later."

Her eyes flew back to his.

Trust the man.

She had been relaxing, and now she was tense again.

"Stop picking on me. I'm not ready for you to tease me about that yet."

"I wasn't teasing," he said calmly, lifting the lid, allowing a big cloud of steam to escape.

"That smells amazing," he said, leaning in and sniffing.

"It does. But I'm not sure I can eat any."

"Why not? The girls told me to come with a big appetite."

"They said that to me too, and I was hungry, but I guess I would rather talk and get it out of the way. It's kinda crazy to me that you can eat when we have something so serious to talk about."

"Would you rather I starved to death while we're discussing it?" he asked, his hand pausing as he lifted the spoon to get some chicken.

"No. I definitely don't want anything to happen to you."

"I think that's a good sign," he said, sounding like he really wasn't sure.

"It is," she said. "Would you mind getting me some?"

He put some on her plate, and she had to admit it looked as good as it smelled.

"So I wonder why the girls did that?" she said, shaking her head and talking almost to herself. She was going to have a huge talk with those girls when they got home. This whole thing was just crazy. Only inviting Elias and then putting the Marry Me Chicken sign on top of the dish and then running off. It was just nuts.

"Maybe they like me. Maybe they want me to hang around?" Elias said with a grin.

"I think I'm seeing a little glimpse of the Elias that you used to be."

"I don't know if I want to bring the whole man back, but I definitely feel like being in Sweet Water has been good for me." He paused, after putting a scoop of chicken on his plate. "Actually, being with you has been good for me. You...have brought out a side of me I didn't realize I had. I like it."

"What side of you?"

"I smile more when I'm around you."

"Really?"

"There you go again."

"Oh my goodness. Are you serious? I make you smile? Mostly because you're making fun of me, right?"

"No. You make me smile because you're funny, cute, and because you're a pretty good kisser too."

"Pretty good?" she asked, insulted.

"Yeah. Pretty good. I don't know, I think with a little practice, you might be really good."

"Oh. With practice. I see. I wonder who I should practice on?" she said, tilting her head as she looked at her chicken, like she was really considering.

"You better watch it. Some people take kissing pretty seriously."

"Do they?"

"They sure do. They might take it so seriously that they think that once you kiss them, that means you're interested in marrying them. And once that happens, they're really hard to get rid of."

"Well, now. That sounds dangerous."

They grinned at each other, and she felt peace settling down in her soul. He had not been scared off when she had gotten scared. In fact, it almost seemed like it had made him stick tighter. To work harder to let her know that she wasn't going to be able to get rid of him that easily. She looked at him.

Together, they stuck their forks into their chicken and took a bite.

It took a little bit, for her to chew and swallow, but she had to talk.

"That is the best dish I have ever eaten in my entire life," she said, and she knew it was crazy, but her voice almost sounded reverent.

"I am right there with you. This is crazy good."

"I was thinking when I saw the sign, I thought it was a dish to get you to want to marry me. But I'm kind of feeling like it's probably a dish to get you to fall in love with chicken."

He laughed, and she loved listening to it. "That's why I love you. Because you are hilarious. And sweet."

"You love me?"

"I guess it took me a while to figure that out, but yeah. I mean, I think that love is more than attraction, and I definitely have that. But as I thought about it, I couldn't think of another woman in the world I would rather spend my life with. Couldn't think of anyone kinder or more compassionate. Someone who makes me laugh and takes life so easily. I... I want to be around you. I want to wake up to your smile and go to bed holding you. I don't want to have to fall down on the sidewalk, pushed by some dumb steer, just to get my arms around you.

I want it to be a daily thing. A multiple times each day thing." He looked down. "That wasn't exactly the way I wanted the words to come out, and I thought it would be a good idea to wait until after we were done eating, but it's the truth."

"They were beautiful words. I'm glad you said them. I... I totally misunderstood what you were saying after we kissed. I thought you said you wanted to talk about it, that you didn't exactly regret it, but I just thought you were going to tell me that it didn't mean what I thought it meant." She took a breath. "And that hurt. I realized then that I was too deeply in love with you to be able to play that game. I... I was trying to protect myself. I have a business and two daughters I have to take care of. I don't have time to nurse another broken heart."

"I sure hope I never break your heart."

"I don't see how you could. I think you're too honorable for that. I knew that the day you told me about keeping your mouth shut and how it destroyed everything you built. It takes a certain kind of character to be able to do that, and you have it. I admire that."

He grinned. "That's good to hear. Good to hear that something good came out of that. Something better than what I had planned."

She could hardly believe that she was better than his time in the military, but that seemed to be what he was saying. "You're saying you'd rather have me than the career you had planned in the Air Force?"

"That's exactly what I'm saying. I realize now that I could be doing what I wanted to, but I wouldn't have been a good man. A righteous man. I was away from the Lord. It took me losing everything to come back. I think that's what God wanted. And maybe you're my reward, or maybe you're just the one God sent to me to let me know that I might have been giving up something, but I was gaining something so much better."

She grinned and looked back down at her plate.

Their talk faded into silence for a little bit as they ate, chatting occasionally with the easy familiarity they had developed.

She could imagine doing this with her girls at the table, for the rest of her life.

She almost felt like it was too good to be true. That there was some kind of catch.

"You should make this at the diner."

"You know, I hate to say it, but this is almost too good for the diner."

"No. But if it's good and people like it, we should figure out how to package it and ship it places. It could be your signature recipe. Jane's Chicken."

"I think Marry Me Chicken sounds a lot better."

"I don't think you're calling me chicken. But I do think you just asked me to marry you."

"I think you need to check your commas," she said. Then she smiled. "Or not. How about this, 'Marry me, Elias?'"

"You're not getting down on one knee and offering me a ring?" he asked, smiling, and she knew he was teasing her.

"That's so old-fashioned," she said airily.

"So what day did you want to get married?"

"Are you serious? What day, or what date?"

"I really meant what day, but if you have to set a date, we can do that too."

"So you want to set a day?"

"Tomorrow?"

"That's so funny. I was so determined that I was not going to let you in, just an hour ago, and now we're talking about setting a date to get married."

"Is it too fast?"

"Maybe a little."

"Guess when I make a decision, I'm ready to move on it. For me, I know for sure this is where God wants me and that you are who God wants me with. I don't need to wait for any length of time. But if you want to have a big wedding or whatever you want, and you need a plan and time, that's fine too."

"No. I don't need a big wedding. I already had one of those, and it didn't make any difference in my marriage. I think I'd just like something small. You and me and the girls."

"That sounds good to me."

"Next week?"

"All right. Tuesday, since you have it off?"

"Yes," she said, smiling a little, because that was probably going to be their life, planning things around the diner and the day it was closed. Although, maybe they could find themselves a good manager if the diner started making enough money to support that.

"Tuesday sounds good. Maybe we could do it Monday night, so we could have all day to spend together."

"Monday night after the diner closes?"

"Yeah. We'll have to go get the license, but it shouldn't take too long and we should be able to do that sometime soon."

"Well. So less than a week?"

"Yeah. And I definitely think we ought to find out from the girls how they made this, get them to show us, and start testing it out on your diners. I think it's going to be a hit."

"All right. And I guess we'll call it Marry Me Chicken."

"With no commas in it."

"No commas."

Chapter 31

"Wow. What a night," Elias said as he flipped the closed sign on the door and locked it after the last patron had left.

"I'm sorry I lied when I said that Friday nights after football season was over would be a lot slower," Jane said as she came and stood beside him, putting an arm around him.

"It's okay. I'm happy we're busy. Your Marry Me Chicken has been such an amazing hit."

"The girls set up an email address, just for the Marry Me Chicken, so that people can send us orders. They told me that I have fifty to-go orders of the chicken tomorrow to get ready, and that's not including what we need to make for the people who come in the diner."

"I think you're going to have to start paying your daughters."

"I think you're right. And if we keep having business like this, we're going to need the extra help."

"Family is dependable, if only because if you need them, you can go upstairs and get them out of bed."

"That's true," she laughed.

"You're not changing your mind, are you?" Elias said, shifting just a little, putting an arm around her, drawing her to his chest.

"Not on your life. In fact, I wouldn't have been against doing it today. We just couldn't get away in order to get the license."

"What do you think about living above the diner for a while, but if things keep going well, we'll build a house out on the ranch?"

"Sweet Briar Ranch?"

"Yeah. With my crew. Some of them anyway."

"They're okay with that?"

"Yeah. There were actually four parcels of land that we bought together. They all went with the property. And we had first choice when we made the offer on the house."

"I see."

"One of them's mine. You don't build a house in a day, but I thought that might be something you and I could do. Again, if things go well."

"Yeah. It...might be a little bit difficult to raise children in the apartment."

He froze for a moment, then looked at her carefully. "I thought you said you didn't think you wanted children?"

"I said I didn't want children with a man that I wasn't sure was going to be around to help me raise them. I... I'm sure about you."

"That's a good thing. Because I'm sticking around. You're going to have a hard time getting rid of me."

"I don't think I'm going to try." She looked up into his eyes, looking forward to Monday, and while she was a little bit nervous, she was more excited than anything. "You said I was the best thing that happened to you and that God rewarded you for giving up everything that you had?"

"Yeah?" he asked, nuzzling her ear.

"Well, I just want you to know that you are an answer to a prayer for my girls. They've been praying for a really long time for a husband for me and for a father for them. They confessed as much to me, and I was afraid a little bit to tell you because I didn't want you to think that I was manipulating you or something."

"You're not a manipulator. We don't have to worry about that anyway."

"I guess it's just one of the things my ex-husband complained about me. I was trying to manipulate him into giving up his friends or giving up something he wanted, and it really wasn't true. I just wanted him to spend more time with me."

"Well, you're going to have a hard time getting rid of me. And that's the truth."

Elias bent his head down and touched his lips to hers, and she forgot about the work they still had to do and just enjoyed the feeling of being with the one who God had given her. The one who was perfect for her.

Enjoy this preview of Just a Cowboy's Secret Baby, just for you!

Just a Cowboy's Secret Baby

Chapter 1

Darby parked her car along the road, down the street from the only diner or place to get food in Sweet Water, North Dakota.

She wasn't sure whether this was a good idea or not, but she had committed, and now she was here.

"What are all those people doing standing around that store?" her daughter, Amber, asked from the back seat.

"I'm not sure. That's where I was planning on eating lunch, before we started looking around town."

"I'm hungry," Amber stated, which didn't surprise Darby. She was hungry too.

"Maybe they have some kind of sale going on or a popular recipe." She spoke, but mostly to herself. She hadn't heard or read of anything going on in Sweet Water today.

It was one in the afternoon. She wouldn't have expected a small-town diner to be so busy, but there were people milling around outside and looking in the windows. The door stood open, and a line snaked out. The odd thing about it was all the people moving around seemed to be women.

She might have thought maybe the local news station was holding an interview in the diner or some such thing like that, but that didn't explain why she didn't see any men around.

"Well, I guess we'll walk over and see if they're still selling lunch. And if not, I suppose we'll need to find somewhere else to eat." There wasn't any place else to eat in town, unless one counted the baked goods offered at the used bookstore. Eating was her excuse to linger, since she really had very little reason to be in town.

Well, it was a big reason to her.

She was looking for her daughter's father.

"Come on. Let's go see what we can find out." She opened her door, getting out and grabbing her purse.

Amber climbed out more slowly from the back seat. At eight years old, Amber wasn't quite old enough to understand that Darby wasn't just taking a joyride while on vacation. Although she knew Darby had sold her catering business and they were looking for a place to put down roots, as Darby had explained it to her.

She didn't know all the reasons why.

She also didn't know that the man who was her father lived in this town according to the information that Darby had been able to look up.

Which wasn't much.

He actually lived outside of town on a place called the Sweet Briar Ranch.

Darby was not familiar with North Dakota. She wasn't familiar with the West at all, being from Maryland.

She hadn't left Maryland for the sole purpose of finding Amber's father, but since she had to leave for Amber's sake, she thought she should look for Amber's father before she settled down anywhere else.

She didn't like the feeling of not having roots, of just drifting. She wanted to have a plan and live out her plan. She didn't want to just rely on God to show her the next step. She wanted to see the entire path from here to eternity.

That wasn't usually the way life worked out. And it definitely wasn't the way God usually worked. He wanted a person to take a step and then stand in faith until it was time to take another.

Sometimes the standing in faith was harder than taking steps.

"Mom?"

"Yes?" she said to her daughter absently.

"Is that...a woolly mammoth?"

Darby glanced at her daughter, bemused. North Dakota might be a little strange to them, but it wasn't like they had gone back in history.

She looked where Amber pointed, and her mouth dropped open.

"It does kind of look like one, doesn't it?" she asked, edging closer to her daughter and putting one hand in front of her as though to protect her.

"Do you think it's going to hurt us?"

"It's coming this way. I don't know if it's friendly. But a lot of times, animals will chase things that are running, so I don't want to run away."

They'd only walked a few yards from her car, but there was a bench on the sidewalk that was closer, so she walked, slowly and as carefully as she could in a state that was starting to feel a lot like panic, to the back of the bench and stood behind it, watching the animal draw closer.

"He looks friendly," Amber said.

"Yes, he does, doesn't he?"

It was true. What she could see of his eyes seemed calm and gentle, but she never took a risk when it came to her daughter.

"I don't think we should assume he is. You don't just go around petting strange cows." She thought it was a cow. She'd never seen one with quite that much...fur? Hair? She wasn't sure. But the horns he sported looked an awful lot like the horns on cows she'd read about in the Old West. Longhorns, they were called.

She didn't remember them having long, shaggy hair on them.

This one wasn't very tall. She'd always pictured longhorns as being much bigger.

The animal moseyed closer, stopping on the other side of the bench and seeming to look at them with those liquid gentle eyes.

Those horns were wicked.

Also, tigers had cute eyes, too. She'd looked at them often in the Baltimore Zoo and aquarium where she and Amber had spent many afternoons. They looked so cool, so sweet and cuddly.

They were wickedly dangerous.

There was no way she was going to assume that this beast in front of them was harmless, not with her daughter's life at stake.

"Mom, I think he wants us to pet him," Amber said, pulling at her hand, which Darby had gripped as she'd pulled her daughter behind the bench.

"Maybe he wants to eat us," Amber said, not in a scared tone but in a conversational tone. At least she hoped she kept the fear out of her voice

"Don't be silly, Mom. Cows eat grass."

"Maybe we've met the one cow in the entire United States who wants to expand his palate."

"Mother. You're being ridiculous."

Her daughter's vocabulary was much larger than a normal child's. That wasn't exactly the reason she'd left Maryland, but it was one of them. Her daughter had another special ability that had necessitated their flight from her home state.

"I'm just being a mom. I'm doing my job, which is to protect you. I don't know for sure whether this cow is dangerous or not, and those horns are huge. While you're almost certainly right that he's benign, if you're not correct, we have more to lose than if I am inaccurate in my observations of the situation."

"Mom, you talk like that when you're scared."

She was right. She had a tendency to be a lot more formal when she was trying to hide something, like fear, or anger, or frustration.

"I'm sorry. But while this beast seems to be harmless, we can't know for sure." She held on tight to her daughter's hand with one hand and made a shooing motion with her other hand. "Shoo. Go on. Get out of here."

The animal looked at them, then shook its head.

Darby jumped back, yanking her daughter with her.

She almost felt foolish, but then the animal looked at them, stretched out its neck, and made the biggest, most ghastly, and frightening noise that Darby had ever heard.

It felt like her eardrums were going to burst.

She grabbed her child more closely to her, hugging her next to her side while keeping both of her frightened eyes on the beast in front of her.

"I'm sorry, ma'am. I'm assuming this car with the out of state tags is yours. Billy here must have noticed we had someone new in town and came to welcome you folks to North Dakota."

A man, dressed in cowboy boots, worn blue jeans, a belt buckle as big as Texas right in the center of his belly, and a button-down shirt with the top two buttons unbuttoned and the sleeves rolled up to the elbows, spoke behind her. Completing his ensemble was a cowboy hat that hid half the man's face. She couldn't quite see what color his eyes were, but the jaw that stuck out from underneath it was covered in stubble and looked to be square and hard.

"Billy?"

"That's our steer." The man's voice held humor. A shiver traveled up her spine. "Sweet Water's own mascot. He doesn't usually welcome strangers. In fact, he usually shies away. But I guess he saw you coming and figured your daughter here would love to pet him."

The man grinned at Amber, who grinned back up at him.

"Really? You mean I could really pet him?"

"Sure can. He's gentle as a lamb. As long as your mom says it's okay."

"Are you sure?"

"Sure as shooting. When the town has festivals, which is pretty much every other week, Billy always gets rounded up and put in a makeshift petting zoo and the kids sit on his back, hang on his horns, and crawl over him. He loves it."

"That's crazy," she couldn't help but say.

"I think, if you're actually from Maryland, and this is your first time in North Dakota, that's going to look pretty normal once you see the rest of the stuff these North Dakota folks do."

"You're talking like you aren't from North Dakota, and yet you sound like you are," she said, noticing the way he interchanged his third- and first-person pronouns.

"I've lived here for not quite two years, and I got acclimated pretty well. And by that, I mean that I survived two winters and feel like I should earn some kind of major award for that."

She laughed. "That's the sign that you've acclimated to the state? Surviving the winter?"

"I don't know how long you're staying, but if you're here in January, you'll feel like you need a badge of honor too if you make it through the month."

"I'm not sure if we're staying or not," Darby said, liking this man, who told it like it was and who seemed friendly but not in her face, gave her enough space to make her feel comfortable.

"Mom, can I pet the cow?"

"It's actually a steer," the man corrected Amber. She liked that he didn't treat her like a little kid but acted like she was capable of rational thought.

So many men didn't know how to act around children.

"I suppose if the man... I guess we should introduce ourselves," she said a little uncertainly. She wasn't used to meeting strange men on the street and handing out her name like candy. But Sweet Water seemed like a friendly place and a lot different from Baltimore. Plus, the man had been kind.

That didn't mean she trusted him. It just meant she was going to introduce herself.

"I'm Darby, this is my daughter, Amber." She held out her hand.

The man took it. His hands were rough, strong, and his grip firm.

"I'm Jonah Mills."

Darby gasped.

Her train of thought was a little derailed because she wasn't expecting his grip to make jolts of electricity shoot up her arm. Unexpected, but not unpleasant.

As he stepped a little closer, she could see under the brim of his hat to the deep brown eyes shadowed there. Serious, but with laugh lines crinkling the corners.

Her eyes caught on his, and their hands remain clasped even after they stopped pumping.

This was the man. Amber's father.

Her shock was still great, her complete surprise at...not just finding the man, and finding him the moment she got into the town, but that she would feel...whatever it was that she felt while touching him. An odd sensation, and even odder when combined with her inability to tear her eyes away from his.

"Mom! Are you gonna let him help me pet Billy?" Amber's voice broke into her consciousness, and she couldn't believe she'd almost forgotten she had a daughter, let alone that they were standing on a street in the middle of a North Dakota town, and there were other people in the world.

She yanked her hand away, embarrassed, backing up. "Of course. He said it was okay, just be careful."

The man, Jonah, seemed to look at her, study her, for another few moments that felt like a really long time before he turned to Amber with an easy grin on his face. "You can come on around the other side of the bench. I promise you, Billy is as tame as an animal gets. He loves attention."

Amber went around, standing trustingly beside Jonah as she followed his example and put her hand on the steer's fur.

"In Sweet Water, we like to think that Billy is a bit of a matchmaker. He's had a hand in getting several local couples together and has started to get himself quite a reputation. Local legend has it that Billy is the way he is because he has an unrequited love for the town pig, Munchy. Munchy doesn't want to have anything to do with Billy, so in order for Billy to feel better about himself, he helps other people who are looking for love get together."

Darby laughed and rolled her eyes at the silliness of Western towns. "Sounds to me like Sweet Water's desperate for tourism dollars."

"Well, that's the funny thing, we haven't really announced it to the outside world. Only people here in Sweet Water get to find out about Billy the steer who thinks he's Cupid."

"Maybe you're right about those North Dakota winters, and they kind of make people a little crazy in the head." She spoke, hoping her voice sounded a little bit reasonable.

She hadn't really gotten off on a very good foot with this man, and she was here hoping to have a working relationship with him. But she just couldn't let the idea of a steer who wanted people to find love go without making fun of it just a little.

"Laugh if you want to. There are several people in town who are married because of this old boy," Jonah said, petting him. He looked over his shoulder at her. "You can come on over and give him a pat if you want to."

Darby wasn't very interested in petting the steer, but she always tried to lead by example with her daughter, and while her daughter was already scratching the animal like she'd been doing it for years,

Darby thought it would be best for her to do it as well, just to let her daughter know that it was good to not give in to your fear.

Pick up your copy of Just a Cowboy's Secret Baby by Jessie Gussman today!

A Gift from Jessie

View this code through your smart phone camera to be taken to a page where you can download a FREE ebook when you sign up to get updates from Jessie Gussman! Find out why people say, "Jessie's is the only newsletter I open and read" and "You make my day brighter. Love, love, love reading your newsletters. I don't know where you find time to write books. You are so busy living life. A true blessing." and "I know from now on that I can't be drinking my morning coffee while reading your newsletter – I laughed so hard I sprayed it out all over the table!"

Claim your free
book from Jessie!

Escape to more faith-filled romance series by Jessie Gussman!

The Complete Sweet Water, North Dakota Reading Order:

Series One: Sweet Water Ranch Western Cowboy Romance (11 book series)

Series Two: Coming Home to North Dakota (12 book series)

Series Three: Flyboys of Sweet Briar Ranch in North Dakota (13 book series)

Series Four: Sweet View Ranch Western Cowboy Romance (10 book series)

Spinoffs and More! Additional Series You'll Love:

<u>Jessie's First Series: Sweet Haven Farm (4 book series)</u>

<u>Small-Town Romance: The Baxter Boys (5 book series)</u>

<u>Bad-Boy Sweet Romance: Richmond Rebels Sweet Romance (3 book series)</u>

<u>Sweet Water Spinoff: Cowboy Crossing (9 book series)</u>

<u>Holiday Romance: Cowboy Mountain Christmas (6 book series)</u>

<u>Small Town Romantic Comedy: Good Grief, Idaho (5 book series)</u>

<u>True Stories from Jessie's Farm: Stories from Jessie Gussman's Newsletter (3 book series)</u>

<u>Reader-Favorite! Sweet Beach Romance: Blueberry Beach (8 book series)</u>

<u>Cowboy Mountain Christmas Spinoff: A Heartland Cowboy Christmas (9 book series)</u>
<u>Blueberry Beach Spinoff: Strawberry Sands (10 book series)</u>